THE
PINKERTON
AND THE
WIZARD

HARVEY HETRICK

THE PINKERTON AND THE WIZARD

iUniverse books may be ordered through booksellers or by contacting:

iUniverse
1663 Liberty Drive
Bloomington, IN 47403
www.iuniverse.com
1-800-Authors (1-800-288-4677)

ISBN: 978-1-6632-0089-1 (sc)
ISBN: 978-1-6632-0090-7 (hc)
ISBN: 978-1-6632-0088-4 (e)

Library of Congress Control Number: 2020910743

Print information available on the last page.

iUniverse rev. date: 06/19/2020

CONTENTS

THE ABDUCTION

Merlin Pendragon looked up from his open spell book through tired eyes and stared pensively at the red lion on a tapestry on one of the lifeless gray walls that surrounded him. Light streamed in from a single open window and touched a faded ornate carpet, which somewhat seemed to offset the room's drabness. He tugged at his tapered beard and wondered why Dagda, the great Celtic god, had chosen him to be King Arthur's mentor. Even though he'd been given the ability to perform great magic, he also realized that he'd have to use it carefully. He'd seen how others had sought power and greed over honesty and compassion. Instead, he wanted to use his magic for good, not personal gain. Unfortunately, he regretted that he'd shared his knowledge of the magic with Morgana, an evil sorceress who seemed intent on using it for evil purposes. With no way to impede her, he could only hope to maintain some balance between his good and her evil. He wondered what her next despicable act would be.

Gwen had listened to the warnings of Merlin, her husband, about the dangers of traveling alone in the forest—even those paths near Camelot itself. She knew that many feared Merlin's powers, while others envied him. Unfortunately, with his unrelenting need to protect her, Gwen's life became more constrained and less enjoyable. As a result, she had few opportunities to venture outside his sphere of concern. She needed to experience nature for herself, without the usual entourage of guards around her.

Early one morning she seized the opportunity to venture outside the walls of Camelot while Merlin busied himself with making his potions. Her rustic cart creaked with each jolt as her horse plodded along a seldom-traveled path. An occasional dogwood bordered the path, and a canopy of oak and elm shaded it. A damp crispness filled the morning air. The chirping of sparrows, the cooing of doves, and the fresh scent of forest vegetation and wildflowers surrounded her. Nothing seemed the least bit threatening.

The faint babbling of a nearby stream caused her to halt her cart. She climbed down from the cart and skirted around several shrubs until she spotted a large smooth boulder bordering the stream. She sat on the boulder, scooped up a handful of water, and sipped it. She then scanned the foliage around her until her gaze latched on to something wondrous. She blinked her eyes several times and stared at a lone bush of incredible black roses surrounded by delicate spider lilies. No one truly thought the black rose actually existed, but here it spread its velvety black petals—a captivating image of awe and splendor.

The rustle of shrubbery behind her startled her. When she turned around and saw nothing, she paused with a sigh of relief before turning back to the stream. Without warning, something stung her in the neck. When she reached to her neck, she touched a feathery object. Within seconds, her body tilted to the side and fell from the boulder.

Morgana watched Fritz lower his blowpipe and insert it into a side pocket in his robe while a broad grin stretched across his narrow face.

"Excellent," Morgana said. "The first stage of my plan is complete."

"What do we do now?" Fritz asked.

"Do you remember that remote grotto I showed you before we followed her here?"

"Yes, of course."

"I want you to put her in her cart and follow me there." Morgana then swirled her long black cloak and returned to her own cart.

Upon reaching the grotto, with Fritz close behind, she went inside the cavernous structure to inspect it in more detail. The limestone ceiling extended well above her head, and the walls formed a large semicircular chamber. A ledge at the back of the chamber resembled an altar perhaps used by some ancient religion.

She formed a devious grin with her thick lips, and her dark eyes leered with a piercing, almost mesmerizing, intensity as she thought about eliminating Merlin. Since she believed her skills had reached a level equal to his, she considered Merlin her greatest obstacle to power.

When Fritz arrived, Morgana glared at the unconscious Gwen. "Carry her to the back of the grotto and put her on that ledge."

"Are we just going to leave her here to die?" Fritz asked.

"Patience," Morgana said. "I have another special task for you."

She waited for Fritz to lumber with long-legged strides back to the grotto entrance after placing Gwen on the ledge. "I want you to bring Merlin to the grotto. Tell him that his wife is ill and that you were afraid to move her too far in her cart."

By afternoon, Merlin arrived and rushed into the grotto, where he saw Gwen lying motionless on the ledge. He touched her cheek and then her forehead, and finally he pried one of her eyelids up. After releasing her eyelid, he reached into his robe and retrieved a small vial. When he opened the vial and passed it beneath her nose, he saw her blue eyes pop open as she began coughing. He raised her to a sitting position, brushed her gray hair aside, and lightly touched her cheek again as she gave him a faint smile.

"I don't know what happened," Gwen said. "I … I just felt so strange."

Merlin saw the feathery protrusion in her neck and removed it. He then spun his head toward the grotto entrance. "What foul treachery is this?" he demanded. He saw Morgana step into view at the grotto entrance.

"This is the end for you, Merlin!"

The earth at the grotto entrance instantly began to heave. Thick vines burst skyward toward the top of the entrance like equally spaced prison bars. Each stalk then began to sprout thick leaves.

"Never again will you interfere with my plans, Merlin!"

Merlin pointed his wand at the vines, but their growth continued. Darkness slowly began to consume the interior of the grotto. He then noticed a nearby boulder and pointed his wand at it. A lightning bolt flashed from the end of his wand to the boulder. As the boulder began to glow with an eerie luminescence, the grotto became illuminated once again.

"What's wrong?" Gwen asked. "Why couldn't you stop the vines?"

Merlin shook his head. "I just can't cancel this particular spell while in the grotto."

"There must be something you can do!" Gwen said.

Merlin tugged at his white beard and stared at the vines through small squinty eyes partially covered by his hat's floppy bill. His bulbous nose extended over a roundish mouth. However, his frumpy appearance, with a cone-shaped hat resting awkwardly on his white hair, didn't instill much confidence. After several minutes of meditation, he released the grasp on his beard and snapped his head toward Gwen. "I think I have it, but it may shock you."

"But will it get us out of here?" Gwen asked.

Merlin didn't respond but closed both eyes. The seconds seemed like minutes, the minutes like hours. Finally, his eyes fluttered open, and he looked around the grotto as if he'd been on a long trip and didn't recognize anything.

"Merlin," Gwen said. "I'm here."

Merlin slowly rotated his head toward Gwen. The glassy stare soon faded. He looked into Gwen's eyes, touched her cheek, and smiled at her.

"What did you see?" Gwen asked. "Did you find a way out of here?"

"I saw the future," Merlin said. "I saw my family's lineage in a man of science in the nineteenth century."

"What does that have to do with escaping the grotto?"

Merlin cleared his throat. "We're going to time travel to the nineteenth century."

"You can't be serious!" Gwen said.

"It's the only way—unless you want to die in here."

"I just hope you're right."

Merlin moved his wand in a large circular motion, and a large shimmering disk appeared in front of him. "Don't be afraid. It won't hurt you. I only need to touch it with my hand for us to leave this entombment."

"I don't know if I'm ready for this. Are you sure it's safe?"

"Of course, but first we need to see how we should be dressed." Merlin touched the disk with his wand. A busy nineteenth-century street scene appeared on the disk. "What's your favorite color, Gwen?"

"I think it's blue. Yes, of course it's blue."

Merlin swirled his wand above their heads. He now saw Gwen in a light blue dress, wearing light brown shoes. He sported a tan suit with a matching vest, a white shirt with a gray tie, black shoes, and a light gray derby hat. After giving his handiwork a cursory review, he then took Gwen's hand and touched the disk.

CHAPTER 1

THE ARRIVALS

Time traveling brought Merlin and Gwen to nineteenth-century Philadelphia, which looked dramatically different from the medieval world. It had broad streets, perfectly aligned buildings, and wooden boardwalks. Many of the buildings looked similar, while others varied in height and color, but all had solid peaked roofs instead of thatch. In addition to these differences, each group of closely spaced buildings contained various businesses with large signs above the doorways to identify them.

Merlin looked up at the Baker Street Bookstore and saw a two-story white clapboard building with a green door, light green shutters, and pairs of adjacent windows on either side of the door. To the left, he saw a similarly constructed building called Broussard's Restaurant and Pastry Shop, and to the right, he saw another called Hulbert's Tailor Shop.

"Do you think your future relative lives in one of these buildings?" Gwen asked.

"I'm certain of it," Merlin said. "It has to be the bookstore. Where else would a person of science acquire knowledge?"

"I see in one of the windows a sign about rooms for rent," Gwen said. "Do you suppose we should rent one? We do need a place to stay."

"I agree, but we need a way to pay for the room."

"But we only have the clothes we're wearing," Gwen said. "What are we going to do?"

"I fully anticipated this," Merlin said. He reached into one of his coat pockets and pulled out a handful of gemstones. "I made a slight addition to my wardrobe during our transformation."

"Do you think they'll accept them for payment?"

Merlin scanned the buildings on the other side of the street until he saw Ballantine's Jewelry Store. "Probably not, but I think our answer may be across the street. Perhaps I can sell some of the gems for the money that's used in this century."

With paper money now in his vest pocket from the gemstone transactions, Merlin entered the bookstore after Gwen and saw rows of freestanding bookshelves filled with books in the center of the room. Against the sidewalls, he saw more bookshelves, and against the back wall, he saw even more bookshelves, interrupted by only a single closed door. He approached a counter near the front door and saw an average-sized man with a waistline betraying a slightly overweight condition. The man's long gray hair surrounded the bald top of his head, and his light brown eyes peered over wire-rimmed glasses. Below a prominent nose, his thin lips formed a narrow mouth.

"May I help you?" the man asked.

Merlin studied the man's face to discern any facial characteristic that might be relevant to his ancestry, but he just couldn't be sure. He had to trust his instincts until he actually had an opportunity to touch the man. Then his magic would confirm it. "Yes, we saw your sign concerning rooms for rent. Might there be a room available for my wife and me?"

"Certainly. I think I can arrange that," the man said. "By the way, what's your name, sir?"

Merlin extended his hand and felt the tingle in their handshake, which confirmed his ancestral connection. "I'm Merlin Pendragon, and this is my wife, Gwen. You can just call me Merlin."

"I'm glad to meet you, Merlin. I'm John Kent. You can just call me John."

"It looks like you have a very fine shop, John. Have you been in business long?"

"Well, not too long. I'm a retired physician, and this is where I decided to retire. I own the bookstore, and I live on the first and second floors in the back half of the bookstore with my wife, Ann, and my son, Lee. Your room will be on the second floor, above the front half of the bookstore. We'll also offer you meals as part of your rent."

"That would be jolly good, John."

"From your accent and your choice of words, you must be from England."

Merlin touched his fist against his mouth momentarily. He always did this at the beginning of a lie. "Actually, we just immigrated to America. I'm now a retired teacher. We wanted to see this wondrous country for ourselves."

"What brought you to Philadelphia?" John asked.

"No particular reason. My father was a successful businessman who left me a comfortable inheritance. I felt it was time to leave England after his passing. Our travels about America finally led us here."

"I also need to let you know that another tenant will be living across the hall from your room," John said. "His name's Adam Blake. He's a Pinkerton detective. He may not always be having meals with us since solving crimes and arresting criminals keeps him pretty busy."

"I see. How fascinating. I wonder if he wouldn't mind sharing some of his experiences with me," Merlin said.

"You might increase your interest in detectives by looking at a short story in this magazine from London. It follows the adventures of a fictional English detective named Sherlock Holmes."

Merlin took a copy of the latest issue of the *Strand Magazine* from John. "Well, thank you, John. I think I will."

CHAPTER 2

A BROKEN PROMISE

One day Adam Blake, the Pinkerton detective, met with Tim Danvers, his longtime partner, in the Pinkerton office of Charles Covington, their supervisor. Adam saw nothing unusual in the office except for the large oval replica of a Pinkerton badge attached to the front of the supervisor's oak desk. A large portrait of Allan Pinkerton hung on the wall immediately behind the desk. On either side of the portrait, he saw portraits of William and Robert Pinkerton, Allan Pinkerton's sons. Each son now shared half of his father's detective agency after their father's passing. As for Charles Covington, Adam saw him as a man surprisingly fit for his age, with wide shoulders and a narrow waist. Even though his red hair had grayed into a golden color, his eyebrows retained their deep red hue. His light blue eyes complemented the color of his hair, and a thick reddish mustache covered his upper lip.

"I have a new assignment for the two of you," Charles said. "It's to protect a payroll transfer from Philadelphia to Chicago for the Acme Mining Company on a train leaving this afternoon."

"Will there be other detectives to assist in the transfer?" Adam asked.

"Yes. There'll be two other Pinkerton detectives on the train. As usual, we try to keep these transfers secret, but you can never be totally certain that the information hasn't been leaked. All I can say is to stay alert and take care of each other."

When a carriage arrived, they started home to pick up their traveling valises before going to the train depot. Adam didn't say anything during the carriage ride. He tried to focus on the payroll transfer, but his thoughts kept drifting to Catherine, Tim's twin sister. He had met with Tim and her at dinner one evening. Her stunning beauty and charming personality captured his heart. Between assignments, he spent nearly all his time with her except when she worked as a human-interest reporter for the *Philadelphia Inquirer.*

"This is where I get off," Adam said when the carriage stopped. "My valise is already packed. If you wait a minute, I'll go get it. We can then go by your place."

"You know, you won't see Catherine. I believe she was supposed to interview someone this morning," Tim said.

"I know. There'll be plenty of time to see her when we get back."

Adam arrived early with Tim at the train depot so they could meet with the other two Pinkerton detectives. During the meeting, he agreed with the others to fire three shots in the air in case of an emergency. He then learned that the strongbox with the payroll money had already been loaded into a baggage car just ahead of the caboose. With this in mind, he stayed with Tim in the caboose. The other two detectives sat in the seats of two new John Deere tractors on a flatbed car a few cars behind the coal tender.

Adam stared out of one of the caboose windows after the locomotive had pulled the train from the depot. He looked over at Tim when he heard Tim fold up a newspaper and toss it on an adjacent seat.

"Catherine didn't come home last night," Tim said. "Was she with you?"

"Well, as a matter of fact, she was."

"And?"

Adam looked down for a moment and then back at Tim. "And I asked her to marry me."

"Well, don't keep me in suspense. What'd she say?"

"She said yes."

"Well, congratulations, old friend. It took you long enough. I knew it was going to happen when I saw your eyes glaze over the first time you saw her."

Adam lowered his head one more time when Tim slapped him on the back, but he didn't notice the long white feather Tim covertly wedged into his hatband.

"You know, you're starting to have that married look already. I guess Catherine knew all along that the two of you were meant for each other."

The uneventful trip soon changed when the train reached the notorious Robber's Bend, where multiple train robberies had occurred in the past. Adam noticed that the train's speed began slowing as it headed up a steep incline. He opened the rear door of the caboose and stepped out on the rear platform.

"What's the matter?" Tim asked.

Adam ducked back into the caboose. "We have riders on horseback gaining on us, and they don't look friendly."

"We need to alert the others with the signal we agreed to earlier," Tim said.

"I'll take care of it," Adam said. He fired three shots into the air before closing the caboose door. He then made his way into the baggage car with Tim. They staggered for a moment as the train started around a sharp bend to the right.

"We'll be entering the Wabash Tunnel pretty soon," Tim said.

A few old crates lay stacked at one end of the car. "Let's see if we can make a barricade around the strongbox," Adam said. "At least it'll offer us some protection."

Before the last crate could be put into position, a dull thumping sound on the ceiling progressed to the front of the baggage car. Adam instantly knew what he had to do.

When Adam yanked open the front door, a tall, dark man confronted him. The man tried to point his revolver at Adam, but Adam shoved the man's hand against the doorframe. The revolver fired into the ceiling and then fell to the floor. Adam ducked the man's fist and rammed him with his shoulder. He then tumbled with the man through the doorway and finally forced the man onto the platform of the next car. Unfortunately, the man's fist connected with Adam's chin this time. Adam tried to shake off the blow, but the tunnel's total darkness now engulfed him. Without a point of reference, he couldn't find his sense of balance to pull himself to his feet. Finally, he resolved to just sit on the platform and try to make out where his attacker might be.

A few minutes passed before blinding sunlight illuminated everything again. Adam squinted and held up his hand to block the glare. He then stood up and stared in disbelief when no other cars exited the tunnel after his.

"Go tell the engineer to reverse the train," Adam said to one of the other detectives who'd arrived moments later. He tightened his grip on the stanchions on either side of him while gritting his teeth. How could this be happening?

First a burst of gunfire, then a second round of gunfire, and finally a single gunshot echoed in the distance. Adam dropped his head in despair. "Oh my God, Tim. What have I done?"

The train backed down the track nearly a mile or so before the second baggage car and caboose came into view. The first baggage car recoupled with the second baggage car with a jolt. Adam jumped to the second baggage car platform and found the forward door still ajar. Light and the haze of gun smoke streamed in through an open side door. Tim lay in a pool of blood next to the empty strongbox.

Adam rushed to Tim and raised his head. He saw blood oozing from the corner of Tim's mouth.

"You know, the women are going to be jealous of your hat," Tim said.

Adam took off his hat and saw the white feather. "Another one of your pranks, I see. I knew you had to be up to something."

Tim coughed. "You know I'm too slick to get caught," Tim said. "Besides, it's great fun to watch you be unaware."

Tears began to roll down Adam's cheeks. "I didn't know things were going to go so terribly wrong. Can you ever forgive me?"

"Of course, but now you've got Catherine to take care of."

After he watched Tim's eyes stare with emptiness, he lowered Tim's head and began to cry. His whole life had been shattered. He'd lost a dear friend, and he'd now have to face Catherine. Would she ever forgive him? He'd made a promise to himself to look after Tim, but he'd failed miserably in doing so.

The Chicago train depot had sparse lighting on the passenger platform but had just enough to allow passengers to mill about without difficulty. The usual odors of tar pitch from the railroad ties and the freshly painted surfaces on the depot walls filled the air, as did the ever-present stench of sulfurous locomotive smoke. No passengers waited on the platform at this hour since the last train had departed for the evening.

Adam sat morosely on a bench in a remote corner of the depot. He watched William Pinkerton sit down next to him and then felt the warmth of William's hand on his shoulder.

"It's not your fault, you know."

Adam looked up at William with reddened eyes. "I just can't believe what happened."

"All I can tell you, Adam, is that it was a well-planned robbery that could have happened to any of us."

"But why did it have to be Tim? He didn't have to die. I should have stayed with him."

"We all make decisions based on what we know at the time,"

William said. "You didn't know that the second baggage car and caboose were going to be decoupled."

"I guess so, but now I've got to face Tim's twin sister. I just proposed to her yesterday."

"Dear me, I can't help you with that," William said. "What do you want to do in the meantime?"

"I want to escort Tim's body back to Philadelphia."

"I'll make the arrangements," William said.

Adam lowered his head and placed it between his hands while staring at the planked flooring.

"Are you thinking about quitting the agency?" William asked.

"I don't know. I can't think about that right now."

"Take all the time you need but don't make any rash decisions. The agency still needs good men like you."

Adam raised his head again and looked over at William. "Thank you for coming, sir."

"I'll let Detective Covington know the situation."

Adam saw Charles and Catherine waiting at the Philadelphia train depot as the train arrived. He guessed that Charles had learned about Catherine from Tim's employment records. After the train came to a stop, he stepped on the passenger platform and slowly walked toward them, stopping in front of Catherine. "Can you ever forgive me, Catherine?"

"How could you have let this happen?" Catherine took off her engagement ring and tossed it on the platform. "I never want to see you again!"

"Perhaps it's better if you don't see each other for a while, Adam," Charles said.

Adam didn't say another word but walked over to where the ring lay. He picked it up, rotated it in the palm of his hand without looking at Catherine, and placed it in his coat pocket.

"When can I see Tim's body?" Catherine asked.

"It's being transported to the Simmons Funeral Home," Charles said. "You can view it there."

CHAPTER 3

A DIFFICULT DECISION

A bright, sunny day and the manicured expanses of Meadowlawn Cemetery barely seemed to offset the somberness of the darkly dressed attendees who surrounded Tim Danvers's coffin. Catherine Danvers stood between William Pinkerton and Charles Covington on one side of the coffin, opposite Adam, John, Ann, Merlin, and Gwen on the other side.

Adam didn't look toward Catherine but kept his head bowed, while Catherine seemed to be staring blankly through a dark black veil. He kept trying to think of ways to console Catherine but suspected that her present state of mind wouldn't allow her to accept anything he might say to her. The loss of his best friend and Catherine's estrangement left him with no current path to follow. He wondered what he should do next. Would he ever be able to resume his career as a Pinkerton detective? His self-confidence had been shattered. How would he ever be able to survive the torment that now consumed him?

After the funeral, Adam and the other bookstore residents—except for Lee, who hadn't left school yet—returned to the bookstore. They all entered John and Ann's kitchen and sat down at a large kitchen table. Adam looked at each person at the table and hoped someone would start a conversation, but only silence prevailed. A sudden knock at a side door thankfully broke the silence, and he watched Ann dry her hands on her apron before opening the door. His demeanor lightened when he saw his uncle George and his sister, Ivy, enter the kitchen. He didn't fault them for missing the funeral since he knew that Uncle George had an enormous responsibility managing his circus with the help of Grant Hall, the ringmaster.

"I'm sorry we missed the funeral, but one of the acrobats suffered an injury during a fall," Uncle George said. "We had to accompany him to the hospital to have a doctor check on a lump on his head."

"I do hope he's all right," Adam said.

"We were concerned that he may have suffered a concussion, but the doctor who examined him thinks he'll be okay after a few days of rest."

Adam approached Ivy and gave her a hug. "I'm glad it wasn't you."

"No, I'm fine. It was just a freak accident," Ivy said. "I'm more concerned about you, Adam. You need to accept what happened to Tim. Have you been able to make amends with Catherine?"

Adam had been to Uncle George's Canterbury Circus, which Uncle George had acquired from an old friend in London after the friend passed away. The movement of the circus to Philadelphia excited Adam because he could now watch Ivy perform as an acrobat, but he worried about Ivy's safety since some portions of the act left him breathless. "I terribly miss Tim. As for Catherine, it seems hopeless."

"Do you now have any regrets about becoming a Pinkerton detective, Adam?" Merlin asked. "I've often had challenges in my life, but no one can always worry about what might have been."

"Until now, I always wanted to follow in my father's footsteps as a Pinkerton detective. Now I wonder if I'll ever be able to clear his name and find his killer."

"I'm sorry to hear about your father, Adam," Merlin said. "Tell me about what happened to him. It sounds like you still have issues about him that need to be resolved. I'd be glad to help if I can."

"Well, as I understand it, he was to guard the stairs leading up to President Lincoln's box at Ford's Theatre in Washington. When he took a few steps from his post to aid a fainting woman, the killer must have taken advantage of the opportunity to sneak up the stairs behind him to kill the president. Congress insisted that he be fired for dereliction of duty."

"It sounds as if he was an unfortunate victim of circumstances," Merlin said.

"It nearly destroyed him both emotionally and financially since he didn't think anyone would now hire him."

"That's where I stepped in," Uncle George said. "I was able to get him a job as a security guard at the Hargrove Bank of Philadelphia."

Adam took a deep breath. "Then he was shot and killed during a bank robbery. Before dying, he managed to write the letters *AV* on the bank floor in his own blood. They're probably the initials of the person who shot him."

"Hopefully, there're witnesses both at the theater and at the bank who can help," Merlin said.

"Perhaps," Adam said.

"Have you thought about what you want to do now?" Uncle George asked.

"I'm so depressed right now. I don't know if I can make any rational decisions," Adam said.

"You could come to the circus and work!" Ivy said.

"What would I do there? I have no skills to offer a circus."

"Don't belittle yourself, Adam," Uncle George said. "You have skills most people never attain. You can be my assistant and learn the business as I have. Not only that, but you can be the circus security officer. Around the circus, there're always dishonest people trying to take advantage of good, honest folks. I'm not getting any younger, you know. Besides, who could I trust more to help me than my own nephew?"

"I never thought about it that way. Perhaps it would work. It might give me a chance to learn something new and different."

"What about the agency, Adam?" Uncle George asked.

"I don't know if I could do it anymore. I'm afraid my memory of Tim will always haunt me. In detective work, you can't let anything impair your judgment."

"Maybe you just need a break from it all," Uncle George said. "The circus would certainly offer you a chance to get back on your feet."

"You're probably right. I can't continue feeling sorry for myself. I've got to move on with my life. I need to talk to Charles about taking a leave of absence because I still want to be a Pinkerton. I just need some time to think things through."

"It would be wonderful to have you at the circus, Adam, if only for a short while," Uncle George said. "I've always known that you could do anything you put your mind to. What do you say? Will you join me?"

"How can I refuse?"

"Things have to get better," Ivy said. "You've still got your whole life ahead of you."

"I know. It's just that so much has happened lately. At least I know I have family and friends to help me through it."

"Do you think you and Catherine will ever get back together?" Ivy asked.

"I don't know, Ivy. All I know is that I miss her so much. I wouldn't know how to approach her again. She's been hurt so much, and she blames me for Tim's death. The gap between us has widened so much that I doubt she even wants to admit that I exist."

"You shouldn't totally give up. I'm sure she must truly love you in spite of everything that's happened."

"I hope so, Ivy. I want to believe that time will heal the pain and sorrow that we both have faced."

CHAPTER 4

A LIGHTNING STRIKE

The circus tent billowed and snapped like a whip with each gust of an angry outside wind, and then a lightning flash as bright as the sun briefly illuminated everything. A second or two passed before the inevitable boom of thunder shook the air. The elephants trumpeted in fear, and the lions roared in defiance. A moment later, the chimpanzees screeched excited protests and the horses reared up and whinnied before pawing the earth and snorting.

Adam turned to Uncle George. "I think we'd better cancel tonight's performance. The storm's much too close, and the animals are too jittery."

"I agree," Uncle George said. "I'll tell Grant to make an announcement."

Adam studied the crowd milling about the tent entrance. He

noticed a familiar man he had once encountered as a Pinkerton detective. When the man's face turned toward him, instant recognition flashed in his brain. He pointed his finger. "See that man there! He's a pickpocket! His name's Vance Watts. He's known as 'Pinch' by his criminal friends!"

Before Uncle George could respond, Adam sprinted toward the entrance with the agility of a hurdler, jumping over everything in his path. He saw Pinch pushing his way through the crowd toward the outside.

When Adam exited the tent, rain came down in torrents and scattered the crowd like ants from a mound, but he could still see his prey scurrying away. He slowed to a stop when he realized he couldn't catch him. Lightning then struck at the same instant as an ear-splitting boom. An intense flash illuminated the flagpole at the top of the tent and streaked down the tent's support rope to a tent stake several feet from Adam. The tent stake exploded into a ball of fire, and the shock wave lifted Adam off his feet, slamming him against the soggy ground with an agonizing thud.

Uncle George pushed his way through the crowd a few minute later. He rushed toward Adam's motionless body and knelt down beside him. A police officer blew his whistle and motioned for an ambulance stationed nearby for emergencies at the circus to move in closer. The attendants lifted Adam into the ambulance, and Uncle George climbed in next to Adam before the ambulance left.

At the hospital, Uncle George confronted a doctor leaving the emergency room. "How is he, Doctor?"

"He's alive, but he's in a coma. We won't know anything until he wakes up."

"What happens now?"

"We'll have him moved to a private room, and one of our specialists will examine him. Until then, it's just a waiting game."

Uncle George soon met Ivy in the waiting room. He saw the anxiety on her face.

"How is he, Uncle George?"

"We won't know until he wakes up from a coma." Uncle George took a proffered satchel from Ivy. "What's this?"

"I brought you some dry clothes," Ivy said. "There's no need for you to catch a cold."

"Thank you, Ivy. I'll find a place to change and then we can go to his room."

After a quick change into the dry clothes, Uncle George knocked on Adam's hospital room door.

"Come in," a voice said from inside the room.

Uncle George and Ivy entered the room and saw a doctor leaning over Adam with his stethoscope.

"Any changes, Doctor?" Uncle George asked.

"His nervous system has been severely traumatized. Unfortunately, I can't say with any certainty that he'll ever recover. It all depends on how much damage has been done."

Uncle George held on to Ivy as she began to sniffle. As a retired physician, he dreaded the outcome of Adam's unknown condition. He knew that if Adam had been any closer to the tent stake, he'd have been killed instantly.

"Can we stay with him for a while?" Ivy asked.

"Certainly, but alert the nurses immediately if he should wake up."

Uncle George and Ivy stayed for about two hours, until Uncle George convinced Ivy that they should come back in the morning after they had some rest.

When they arrived the next morning, they found John, Ann, Merlin, and Gwen already in Adam's room.

Uncle George shook John's hand. "How'd you find out about Adam?"

"One of our bookstore customers told us early this morning."

"You're a retired physician, John," Uncle George said. "What do you think of Adam's condition?"

"Well, I've only seen one case like Adam's. I hate to say it, but his prognosis doesn't look very good."

"Do you have any idea what he'll be like when he wakes up?" Merlin asked.

"It's hard to say, but most likely he'll not be able to function normally."

"What should we do next?" Ivy asked.

"I've talked to the attending physician, an old colleague of mine," John said. "I've convinced him to let me take Adam back to the bookstore until he wakes up."

"I think I'd also prefer that," Uncle George said.

"I'm glad you agree since I've already made arrangements with the hospital for the transfer."

"No argument here," Uncle George said.

"Gwen and I can watch him since we're just across the hall from his room," Merlin said.

CHAPTER 5

THE MIRACLE

As promised, Merlin and Gwen began watching Adam after the attendants from the ambulance returned him to his room in the bookstore. Merlin wanted to spare John and Ann the ordeal of having to climb the stairs routinely to check on Adam. As for the room itself, a bay window bracketed by light blue curtains allowed natural light into the room and provided a temporary perch to watch Adam's pale face and mummy-like position on his bed. A painting of a pastoral scene on the wall facing the bay window offered some solace to the gloomy atmosphere. At the end of the room, a single doorway opened into a small clothes closet with shelving on one side. Next to the foot of the bed, a cedar chest nearly extended the width and height of the bed and probably held additional bed linen and a bulky comforter. Merlin had to smile when he saw a small table next to the bed, which held a lamp and a copy of the *Strand Magazine* like the one John had offered him.

"Do you think there's anything you can do for Adam?" Gwen asked.

"I wish I could use my healing cup, but it wouldn't work since Adam is unconscious."

"What's a healing cup?"

"It's something I created for the Lady of the Lake when her nymphs brought King Arthur to the Isle of Avalon to heal his battle wounds. After its use, it disintegrates and disappears, reappearing exactly one year later."

"What's in the healing cup?"

"All I'm going to tell you is that the user needs to decipher the riddle on the side of the cup."

"That sounds like you, Merlin. You never want to share your secrets with me."

"It's not that, Gwen. It's that the revelation of one secret usually leads to another. I don't want to take a chance of my magic leaking out to anyone. I don't know how anyone in this century would react to it. I especially don't want either of us to suddenly be looked at with suspicion and mistrust. Nothing good can come from any of it."

"All right, so you don't have the healing cup. What else can you do for Adam?"

"I'll just have to do it the old-fashioned way," Merlin said with a sigh. He moved next to the bed and placed his hand on the back of Adam's left hand. The two of them began to glow with a strange luminescence for nearly a minute. "It'll be morning before the spell has taken full effect. We'd best let him rest for now. I'd also better try to get some rest myself. The spell took quite a bit of energy from me."

"Will he have any aftereffects?" Gwen asked.

"He'll be just fine physically, but mentally there'll be some differences."

"What do you mean by that?"

"As a benefit to me, our bonding will now allow me to contact Adam's mind whenever it seems necessary."

"I can see how that might be a benefit to Adam as well. You'll be able to help him regain his confidence."

"We'll see," Merlin said. "Just the same, I plan to stay close at hand so I can help him with his crime fighting."

At daybreak the next day, Adam's eyes fluttered open. He stretched, yawned, and then finally sat up. Why did he feel so stiff? How did he get back in his room? He remembered chasing Pinch through the rainstorm but nothing else.

Multiple footsteps coming up the stairs echoed in the hallway outside of the room. He saw John and Ann reach his room and freeze at the doorway.

"It's a miracle!" Ann said.

"It's absolutely astonishing!" John exclaimed. "More than that, it's totally impossible! Maybe I should start believing in miracles too. I don't understand any of this!"

"I feel fine," Adam said. "I'm just a little tired and stiff."

"I want you to rest today," John said. "I'm going to ask the doctor who examined you in the hospital to have another look at you."

"The hospital! Why was I in the hospital?" Adam asked.

"You don't remember, do you?"

Adam gave John a confused look. "Remember what?"

"The lightning! You were struck by lightning."

"You can't be serious," Adam said.

"It was a good thing you weren't any closer to the tent stake that the lightning hit. You're lucky to be alive."

Adam rubbed the back of his neck. His mind struggled with the reality of what he just had been told. "I see what you mean."

That evening, he received a visit from the doctor who had seen him in the hospital. He sat patiently while the doctor examined him and then waited while John and the doctor had a discussion outside his room. The discussion ended when the doctor left and John reentered Adam's room.

"Well, what does he think?" Adam asked.

"We're both still mystified about your remarkable recovery, but we both think you should take it easy for a few days to be sure there're no aftereffects."

Adam stretched again. "I have no problem with that. I've been meaning to take a few days off anyway."

Before Adam could lie back down, Uncle George and Ivy rushed into the room. He gladly accepted Uncle George's hearty handshake and Ivy's hug and peck on the cheek.

"I'm so glad you're all right, son, even though I don't understand what happened to bring you back to health so quickly," Uncle George said.

"Me too," Ivy said.

"I'll be back at the circus before you know it, Uncle George."

"Just don't get too comfortable with lounging around. I'll have plenty of things for you do when you do come back."

"I have a big surprise for you, Adam," Ivy said.

"I don't know how much more I can take in my weakened condition."

"I guarantee you'll like this one."

Adam then saw Edward Frost, his friend from London, appear in the doorway. They had been classmates at University College London, where they both earned their master's degrees in criminology. He later learned that Edward had become a Lloyd's detective.

"I bet you thought you wouldn't see me again, old chap," Edward said.

Adam tried to stand again but decided to ease back on the bed again. With Edward's handshake and firm grasp of his shoulder, he felt reassured of his recovery.

"He looks fine to me," Edward said.

"I'll be even better when everyone stops pampering me."

"Edward even paid for Lizzie and her father to come to America," Ivy said.

Adam remembered how Lizzie Tolbert had trained Ivy in London to be an acrobat and how they had become best friends. As for Edward, he also remembered that Edward and Ivy had become more than just friends.

Adam smiled at Edward. "I see that there's yet another reason for Ivy to be so happy, but why did you and Lizzie decide to leave England?"

"Well, it was really a combination of circumstances," Edward said. "First my dear mother passed away. After I sold her house, I requested a transfer to the Lloyd's Philadelphia office. Several weeks passed before I received approval. When I went to tell Lizzie that I was leaving England, I learned that her father had been laid off. I knew Lizzie loved the Canterbury Circus and wanted to see Ivy again. I also knew that she and her father couldn't afford the fare, so it just seemed natural that I pay the fares for all of us to leave together."

"Lizzie's father, who's a shipwright, thinks he can get a job at the new Bath Iron Works in Bath, Maine," Ivy said.

"Has Lizzie rejoined the circus?" Adam asked.

"Not yet. She's going to stay with her father while he's getting settled," Ivy said.

"There's no doubt in my mind that she'll come back to the circus," Uncle George said.

Adam turned to Edward. "By the way, Edward, I think there may be a room available for you right here at the bookstore."

"Jolly good," Edward said. "I can't think of a better place to stay."

"It's getting late, and I need to get back to the circus," Uncle George said.

"Ivy and I are going to have a little something to eat, and then I'll bring her back to the circus," Edward said.

"Take care, Edward," Adam said. "It's been really good to see you again."

"Same here, Adam."

CHAPTER 6

REFOCUSING

Adam completed his recovery from the lightning strike without any complications. It made him accept his mortality and realize the preciousness of life itself. He didn't want to waste another minute of his life on sorrow, self-pity, or regrets. He needed to accept things for the way they had become and move on with his life. He didn't know of anyone to turn to except John and Ann, who, in a sense, had become his new parents. When he needed guidance the most, he knew they would try to help advise him as best as they could. To find a clear path to his future, he pondered whether Catherine could ever be a part of his life again. He thought Ann might be the best source of information about Catherine.

One morning at breakfast, Adam looked at Ann with anticipation. "Ann, have you saved any old newspaper clippings about Catherine?"

"I think I have some. Why do you ask?"

"I'm just curious."

He watched Ann move to a cabinet next to the stove and remove a wooden box. A handful of clippings soon covered the table.

"Here's one. It says she married Bill Winston, a local attorney. It's dated just a few weeks after Tim's death."

"He must have been an old boyfriend for her to have married so soon after our breakup," Adam said.

"Life goes on, you know, Adam. She must have felt insecure and needed someone to lean on."

Adam sighed. "Too bad it wasn't me."

"Here's another one," Ann said. "Oh dear, I'd forgotten about this."

"What does it say?"

"It says that Bill Winston died after a severe illness a few months after their marriage and just before Catherine gave birth to a child. The child was named Madeline. You have to realize that it's been over a year since you broke up with Catherine."

"A child? Really? I had no idea."

"Somehow, it doesn't seem right for the child to be born without knowing her father," Ann said.

Adam shook his head. "I agree. What a terrible situation for her to face. I can't imagine how she felt losing her husband just before giving birth."

"It takes a strong woman," Ann said. "She's obviously a survivor."

Adam rubbed his chin. "Well, I can certainly tell you that she's strong-willed."

He then thought of Ivy and Edward and the close relationship they enjoyed. He knew it wouldn't be long before they married. He envied them, but envy didn't make his life any better. He wanted to get Catherine out of his mind because he knew she'd never want to be with him. He thought being a bachelor might have its advantages, but it didn't seem to help him avoid the heartache associated with his lost relationship with Catherine. He needed to refocus his energies on something else to take his thoughts in a different direction.

The circus seemed to offer him what he needed. Everyone worked together to create an atmosphere of excitement, anticipation, and enjoyment. He enjoyed most of the things he saw and tried to keep an open mind about what the circus really represented. Some of the things he liked were the incredible human performances by individuals having incomparable skill and a dedication to perfection. As an example, he held his breath each time he saw Ivy propelled twenty feet into the air by a teeterboard to land in an elevated chair held up by a long pole. He instantly recovered when he saw Ivy confidently smile and wave to the audience as if sitting in a comfortable rocking chair.

He also marveled at the trapeze artists who climbed a single rope with only their hands to reach their swings. He saw high-wire artists inch their way onto a narrow rope with long balance poles. Only the large nets below them eased his concerns about a missed handgrip on a swing or a misstep on the high wire. He then saw a performer ejected from a large cannon into the same net.

He became particularly unnerved when he saw a performer running on the outside of one of two cylinders, their axles connected to a large beam with a center support to allow the cylinders to rotate around the support.

He found other acts more disturbing, such as when he saw animals performing tricks that appeared unnatural to their normal behavior. He saw elephants standing on movable round pedestals with barely enough space for their four large feet before standing upright on their hind legs. He saw lions and tigers in large cages being taunted by a tamer's repeated cracks of his whip. With each roar, he anticipated a retaliatory leap in defiance of the whip's power.

Yet he delighted in acts such as the jugglers with their whirling Indian clubs, the seals balancing inflated balls on their noses while passing the ball to other seals, and mischievous chimpanzees cavorting on the backs of trotting horses while performing handstands followed by backflips.

He even briefly imagined himself as a clown tightly packed with other clowns in a small mostly closed carriage drawn by a miniature horse. That image quickly vanished when his fear of claustrophobia took over.

It didn't take much effort for Adam to become easily caught up in the enthusiasm of the performers. He saw a great deal of potential for the circus. Unfortunately, he began noticing quite a few empty seats in the grandstands.

One day, Adam approached Uncle George. "The crowds don't seem to be as big as they used to be, Uncle George. We haven't had a sold-out crowd since we arrived in Philadelphia. Why do you think that is?"

"I've noticed that too," Uncle George said. "It's sometimes hard to know what interests and excites people. I don't think it's our show."

"I don't think so either, but I've got an idea."

"What do you have in mind?"

"I think we need to advertise more. We need large posters placed around the city. The circus parades are just not enough because some people don't see them. We need posters in every city we visit."

"You may be right. In fact, I've got some money set aside for such things."

"Do you know of anyone in the circus who could create the posters, Uncle George?"

"As matter of fact, Ellen Baxter, the wife of one of our roustabouts, is an excellent seamstress who keeps our costumes in top shape. She's also an excellent artist who's created most, if not all, of the artwork around the circus. I've even seen some of her oil paintings. They're excellent."

"I think I've met her once, but I didn't realize how important she is to the circus. She sounds perfect. Do you think she knows any print shops in the area that could actually make the posters and banners that give the location of the circus and the performance times?"

"I'll talk to her, but I don't think it'll be a problem," Uncle George said. "These artist types seem to know each other and what's going on around them."

"What do you think about enlisting the help of some of the boys at the circus to distribute the posters?"

"I think that's an excellent idea. The parents might like the chance to give them something meaningful to do to keep them out of trouble."

"I assume you never got into trouble as a youngster, Uncle George?"

"I'm not going to admit to anything."

CHAPTER 7

ADAM BECOMES A HERO

The late afternoon sun created the shadow of the adjacent building on the floor of Merlin and Gwen's room. Merlin sat in a padded chair and welcomed the quiet in the room so he could clear his mind and ignore any distractions. While Gwen sat quietly in a rocking chair with her knitting, he wondered how he could help Adam with anything he might be investigating. In medieval times, detectives didn't exist. Those suspected of a crime had their fate determined by the king himself, with only the accusations of determined witnesses. A detective's role in this century seemed to require him to delve into the actual evidence of the crime before judgment would be passed. He only knew he wanted to protect his identity and his magic.

On one particular day, Merlin began to tremble while sitting in his padded chair. Just as suddenly as the trembling began, it abruptly ceased, with him returning to normal.

"What happened, Merlin? Are you all right?" Gwen asked.

"Yes, but I had another vision of the future. It's about Adam."

"What did you see?"

"There's going to be an assassination attempt of someone at a theater where Adam, Edward, and Ivy are watching a play."

"Is there any way to stop it?"

"There may be. I'll try to communicate with Adam, but he won't know where the message is coming from." Merlin immediately went into another trance, but without the trembling.

Adam enjoyed the first half of the play at the Broadmoor Theater with Edward and Ivy. During the intermission, he noticed several people stand up in the audience. The noise level of innocent chatter increased dramatically.

He also decided to stand up. "I think I'm going to the lobby to stretch my legs."

He felt fine when he reached the lobby, but he suddenly became disoriented for a few moments. When he came to his senses, he remembered a strange voice in his head telling him what would be happening.

"Fear not," the voice said. "There's one who seeks to harm another. Waste not a moment to deter his actions."

When he saw a suspicious-looking man climbing the stairs to the balcony, he knew he had to do something about what the voice had told him. He started to reach for his revolver but decided not to because he didn't want to startle the people around him and also alert the potential assassin of his presence. Instead, he dashed up the stairs and saw the man entering one of the boxes. When he entered the box, he saw the man raise a revolver. Without hesitation, he charged into the box and slammed into the man. Upon impact, the revolver discharged into the ceiling and fell to the main floor below when the man's wrist banged against the railing at the edge of the box. The man tried to force his way past Adam, but Adam knocked him out with a right cross. Adam then looked down at the intended victim who sat next to the railing.

"You saved my life, son! What's your name?"

Adam shook the man's outstretched hand. "It's Adam Blake, sir."

"Well, I'm Senator Sid Durant. I want to thank you. I'm certainly glad you came along when you did."

A few minutes later, Adam saw Edward and Ivy enter the box as two security guards hauled the assailant away.

"What happened?" Edward asked.

"This young man saved me from an assassin's bullet," Senator Durant said.

Another man huffed and puffed his way into the box, lowering his head to catch his breath. Adam felt sorry for him. After a few gasps, the man pulled open his coat to expose a police officer's badge next to an ugly stain of marinara sauce on his white shirt. He surmised from the officer's girth that he had a robust appetite.

"I'm Inspector Frank Fagan of the Metropolitan Police Department."

"You may recognize me, Inspector. I'm Senator Sid Durant."

"Yes, I did recognize you, Senator, but can anyone tell me what happened?"

"This young man saved me from a would-be assassin," Senator Durant said.

"You look vaguely familiar," Fagan said. "Are you by any chance Howard Blake's son?"

"Yes, I am. My name's Adam Blake."

"I knew your father. He was a fine man. I hope someday his name's cleared. He didn't deserve to be fired after the Lincoln assassination."

"I agree," Adam said. "I plan to clear his name and find his killer."

"I believe you will, but I know one thing your father would be proud of. It would be what you did this evening."

"Thank you, Inspector." Adam left the box with Edward and Ivy. When they reach the lobby, he felt the back of Edward's hand stop him.

"One thing bothers me, Adam."

What's that?"

"How'd you know this was going to happen?"

Adam rubbed his chin. "I really don't know. All I remember is having a strange sensation when I reached the lobby. It was as if someone was speaking to me in my head."

"I don't believe in psychic events," Edward said. "It's just not possible."

Adam pleaded his case. "Psychic or not, something happened to me! Why else would I do what I did?"

"We may never know, but I'm going to keep an eye on you," Edward said. "Have you been getting enough sleep lately?"

"Don't look at me that way. I'm just as normal as you!" Adam looked at the ceiling and touched his chin with his finger. "Except for the lightning strike."

"Yes, the lightning strike," Edward said. "I still haven't figured that one out."

CHAPTER 8

UNCERTAIN CLARITY

Adam pondered his remarkable recovery from the lightning strike and the recent voice in his head. He didn't know if a connection existed between the two events, but the thought of going crazy swirled in his head. How could any of this be happening to him? Would he hear the voice again? What would he do the next time it happened? Who did the voice belong to? None of it made any sense. He finally decided to seek the help of Madame Gisele, the fortune-teller at the circus. He thought she might be the best-qualified person he could think of in matters concerning mysticism. Besides, he'd often gone to her for advice because he trusted her. He knew she based her predictions partially on the questions she asked her clients. She then made blissful suggestions about their future. It probably didn't matter to some about the accuracy of her predictions, but it gave them renewed hope for a brighter future. Nonetheless, he also knew that her least serious clients sought her predictions merely for entertainment.

Madame Gisele's wagon resembled a small house on wheels, with stairs leading up to a platform and a small rear door. Adam rapped on the door but didn't receive a response. He tried again, but still no one opened the door. He finally decided to open it himself. Inside, he saw Madame Gisele and Inspector Fagan sitting on either side of a small circular table. A lantern hung from the ceiling over a large clear glass sphere in the center of the table. "I'm not interrupting anything, am I?"

"Certainly not, Adam," Madame Gisele said. "Please come in."

He saw that she wore a pleated long dress with a high girth, accentuating her slight plumpness. On her head, he noticed that a light blue scarf tightly covered most of her dark hair. Large gold earrings dangled from her earlobes.

He knew that she traveled with the circus in her own wagon, which formed part of a midway just outside the main entrance. He didn't understand Inspector Fagan's presence but saw nothing unusual about it.

"I didn't expect to see you here, Inspector," Adam said.

"Madame Gisele and I are old friends. We were just reminiscing."

"Perhaps I should come back later," Adam said.

"No, no, Adam. Please take my place because I need to go anyway," Fagan said.

"The next time you come, Inspector, I'll fix you a delicious goulash," Madame Gisele said.

"That would be sheer delight. I look forward to it."

After Fagan left and closed the door, Adam sat down at the table. He drew one hand across his cheeks and stared at the globe.

"It's been awhile since I've seen you, Adam," Madame Gisele said. "What's troubling you?"

Adam leaned forward and rested his elbows on the table. He then placed the palms of his hands on the table. "Strange things have been happening to me lately. You remember that I was struck by lightning and then miraculously cured, right? Now I've heard a voice in my head. For some reason, it allowed me to foil an assassination attempt on Senator Durant. Have I experienced something supernatural?"

"The supernatural is a strange thing that nobody really knows anything about, but I do think it exists. Here at the circus, I've met second- and third- generation performers. Some of them actually swear they've seen apparitions of their dead relatives walking the high wire, swinging on the trapeze, or even riding unicycles late at night. Yet these apparitions don't interact with the living. What surprises me about your situation is that something actually does interact with you. It's as if you have a guardian angel that protects you and helps you protect others."

Adam knew that Madame Gisele faked her predictions of the future and her séances with the dead, but could she actually contact the living with only her mind? He had to find out. "Is there any way you can contact this guardian angel? Maybe I could talk to it and find out what it wants."

"I don't know if it's possible. You know that I've never actually used only my mind to contact the living or the dead, don't you?"

"Of course I do, but it doesn't matter. I want to try anyway."

"Very well," Madame Gisele said. "Let's see if it works for you."

Adam rotated his hands upward and grasped her fingertips. Within seconds, he felt a tingle in his fingers as Madame Gisele closed her eyes and took several deep breaths. The table began to shake violently, and a cloud billowed inside the globe. Then the distorted face of a man appeared in the cloud. He saw surprise and fear consume Madame Gisele's now wide-open eyes. He watched her whole body shudder before she released his fingers and slumped backward from pure exhaustion.

Adam now realized that something seemingly tangible had invaded his consciousness, but he still didn't know why. The failed attempt to contact it had left him in a quandary. He had no way to know what it wanted, just that it seemed to protect him and prompt him to do good things. He gladly accepted those good things, but he still wished he had some way of knowing why he had been chosen.

CHAPTER 9

A PARTNERSHIP

Adam and Merlin sat at John and Ann's kitchen table one morning having coffee before Adam left to see his supervisor. Adam enjoyed Merlin's company but really didn't know much about him. He noticed that Merlin spent a considerable amount of time browsing the books in the bookstore. This made him see Merlin as a very intelligent and knowledgeable person, but he wondered what Merlin had done for a living before retiring on his father's inheritance. He sensed a peculiar strangeness about Merlin that he couldn't quite figure out. He didn't seem to be able to put Merlin in any of the molds that most people fit in. Then again, maybe he shouldn't try and should just accept Merlin's uniqueness.

"Would you mind telling me what you did for a living before leaving England?" Adam asked.

"Not at all," Merlin said. "I was a teacher of many things, but mostly I had a passion for understanding the wonders of the world.

It was a very enjoyable profession, and I found it both stimulating and satisfying."

"As for me, I suffered through an advanced degree in criminology, but I think it's served me well," Adam said.

"This business of being a detective fascinates me," Merlin said. "I'm curious to see how you go about collecting evidence and tracking down the elusive criminals. Is there any danger to you from these unsavory characters? I can imagine you being in some unusual predicaments."

"Sometimes, but not usually. I always have a backup in particularly dangerous situations."

"I see," Merlin said. "I assume that it's usually another Pinkerton detective, is it not?"

"That would be the normal case, but since Edward Frost is now in Philadelphia, I would try to have him be my backup. With him being a Lloyd's detective, I'm sure he could be made available if the Lloyd's Insurance Company had a policy on a particular stolen item involved in one of my investigations."

"I'd like to propose something to you, Adam, and I hope you'll take me seriously," Merlin said. "I realize that you've taken a leave of absence from the Pinkertons, but when you do return as an active detective, I'd like to accompany you and Edward, or whomever, during your investigations. I promise that I wouldn't get in the way, but I think I could offer some assistance with my considerable knowledge."

"That's an intriguing proposal, Merlin, but what about Gwen? Would she agree to your being gone for significant periods of time?"

"We've faced separation before. Besides, Gwen and Ann have become quite close at the bookstore. I'm sure they'll find ways to entertain themselves."

"You know, of course, that the Pinkerton Agency couldn't be responsible for your safety."

"I've lived this long, Adam. I've never foolishly exposed myself to danger, and I don't intend to do it in the future."

"I'd like to accommodate you on your proposal, Merlin, but why don't you first accompany me to my supervisor's office? I'd like to get his opinion and consent."

"I agree. That'd be jolly good, Adam."

Adam rapped on the office door of Charles Covington and waited for a response. He looked over at Merlin and tried to imagine how Charles would react to Merlin's proposal. Would he reject it altogether or would he take the more cautious approach and allow it, with a number of restrictions, of course? He just couldn't be sure how it would turn out. He personally didn't think it would be an issue, and he thought Merlin would be a welcome addition to a usually tedious process of interviewing witnesses and collecting evidence. He suspected that Merlin had a calculating mind and might be helpful in unravelling any baffling mystery.

Upon entering the office, Adam saw Charles rise from the chair behind his desk and offer his hand to Merlin. "I'm Charles Covington. I don't believe we've ever met."

"Certainly not," Merlin said. "My name's Merlin Pendragon. I'm a tenant at the bookstore where Adam lives."

"I assume by your accent that you're from England."

"Yes, quite so, but I've taken a liking to this vast country and have decided to stay awhile."

"It's a wonderful country, and it has much to offer," Charles said. "I assume Adam has brought you here for a reason."

Adam interrupted. "Merlin has made a proposal to me, which I would like you to carefully consider."

"I see, and what's the nature of this proposal?"

"He'd like to accompany me on my investigations as a consultant. Having been a teacher, he has considerable knowledge of many subjects. He might be a useful companion to help in areas where I may not have a full understanding."

"Adam has put it very precisely," Merlin said. "I don't mean to impose but merely to assist."

"I understand," Charles said. "I assume Adam has explained to you that we can't assume any responsibility for your safety. Also, we won't be able to offer you any compensation since you're not an employee of the agency."

"I totally agree and accept full responsibility for my own safety."

"Then it's settled," Charles said. "I accept your proposal."

"That's bloody good of you, Charles," Merlin said. "I don't think you'll be disappointed in what I have to offer."

"Of course, Adam, this decision assumes that you've decided to now become an active Pinkerton detective again. Did your leave of absence with the circus help you come to grips with Tim's death and your separation from Catherine?"

"Both are still painful, but the circus and my recovery from the lightning strike have given me a new perspective about my vulnerabilities and how I should move ahead with my like. Yes, I think I'm ready to continue as a Pinkerton detective."

"That's wonderful, Adam," Charles said. "I do think you've made the right decision. As a matter of fact, I have a new assignment that I hope you and your new partner will be able to accept."

"A new assignment? By Jove, that sounds bloody exciting," Merlin said. "What does it entail?"

"Unfortunately, there've been some thefts at the Museum of Archeology and Anthropology. I'd like you, Adam, and of course you, Merlin, to look into them."

"This sounds like something where I could really be useful," Merlin said. "I've read quite a bit about artifacts, you know."

"I'd also like to contact Edward Frost," Adam said. "Lloyd's may have some policies on the stolen items."

"That's an excellent Idea, Adam," Charles said. "By the way, I have someone I want both of you to meet."

Adam watched Charles open a side door leading to an adjacent office. He looked suspiciously at the open doorway and saw someone standing next to a desk.

"Come on in, Dan. I want you to meet these gentlemen."

Adam saw someone tall and thin standing stiffly with an expressionless face.

"Dan, I want you to meet Adam Blake and Merlin Pendragon, a new civilian observer. Adam and Merlin, this is Dan, my son."

Adam showed surprise and shook Dan's hand. "I'm glad to meet you, Dan. I had no idea that Charles had a son."

"It's jolly good to meet you, Dan," Merlin said.

Adam watched Dan lift his head in an aristocratic manner and stand at attention like a soldier. He then listened to Dan speak in a curt, proper manner.

"It's nice to meet both of you."

"Dan attended Marshall Military Academy as a young lad. Unfortunately, he still retains some of that spit and polish that was ingrained into him, but I finally convinced him to join the agency as a detective."

"I don't regret my academy training, Father. It taught me discipline, honor, and respect."

"I'm sure it did, son, but now it's time to ease back into society, where people aren't quite so disciplined."

"If you say so."

"There's something you can do for me, Adam."

"What's that, Charles?"

"I haven't been able to partner Dan with another available detective so he can get some field experience. I'd like you to let Dan tag along with you and Merlin during the investigation."

Adam furrowed his brow. "Do you think that's wise? We could be running into some very nasty people."

"There's no one I trust more with my son than you, Adam."

"I've had all the training, and I'm willing to do whatever you need me to do," Dan said.

"It's true about the training, but I don't want Dan to carry a weapon just yet, until you think he's ready," Charles said. "The academy did a great job of teaching him how to carry a weapon but not when to use it."

Adam looked at Dan's grinning face and rubbed his chin. "I guess I can agree to it."

"I have no objection," Merlin said. "He looks like a good chap. We'll have a rollicking good time of it, don't you think?"

"Be sure you listen to Adam, son."

"Yes, sir, I will."

After a few minutes of waiting for a carriage, they decided to walk down a few blocks since a carriage hadn't passed by for quite some time. On the other side of the street, Adam saw a young woman step from the boardwalk in an effort to cross the street as a carriage sped toward her. He couldn't believe that the woman didn't instantly move back to the boardwalk. Incredulously, he watched Dan dash across the street, snatch her up, and set her down where she had stepped off the boardwalk. In spite of the driver's efforts to slow the carriage, it sped past them moments later.

"Bravo!" Merlin said.

Adam frowned. "I thought it was very foolhardy. He should've tried to flag down the carriage." He then watched Dan talk to her before he walked back across the street.

"Her name's Eva Sims, and she works at the Hargrove Bank."

"That was a very chivalrous think you did, young chap," Merlin said.

Adam became sullen and looked down. He thought about his father.

"What's the matter, Adam?" Merlin asked.

Adam sighed. "It's just that the Hargrove Bank is where my father was killed during a bank robbery."

CHAPTER 10

GRAND THEFT

With its gray brick exterior and narrow portico over double wooden doors, the Museum of Archeology and Anthropology looked much like the other public buildings. Two round stone pillars supported the portico, and floor-to-ceiling windows could be seen adjacent to each pillar. The front of the portico had the engraving MUSEUM OF ARCHEOLOGY AND ANTHROPOLOGY.

A semicircular marble counter greeted visitors a short distance inside the museum. Just behind the counter, a marble wall extended all the way to a vaulted ceiling. A large portrait of a man hung from the lower portion of the wall, with a brass plate just below it reading WILLIAM F. FRANKLIN, SR., FOUNDER. Tall entryways on either side of the wall allowed access into the interior of the museum. Just behind the wall, a single doorway opened into an office. Laura Morgan sat at a desk in the office and finished copying the items on the recent invoices. She then folded the list and discreetly tucked it into her purse as usual on one of those Fridays when new items had arrived at the docks.

Though not as attractive as some women, Laura had a strong, decisive demeanor. Her coarse black hair fell casually to either side of a center part and bracketed an oval face with dark deep-set eyes. She seemed honest for the most part but had no qualms about engaging in less than ethical activities. Her desire for wealth enrichment usually overwhelmed any pangs of guilt or concerns about what others might think.

She left the museum promptly at five o'clock, as she always did at the end of the day. She began walking toward home since she lived only a few blocks from the museum. Occasionally, she stopped at the Bellevue Café on Fridays. On this particular Friday, she entered the café and scanned the room. When she recognized Zack O'Brien, whom she had seen on several Fridays at the restaurant, she moved to his table and sat down opposite him.

"Do you have the list?" Zack asked.

"Of course I have the list. Do you think I'd be here just to be seen with you?" When she took the list from her purse and slid it toward Zack, she felt Zack put his hand firmly on her hand.

"We could make this a little more personal if you want to. We could even meet here on Fridays when there isn't a list."

Laura quickly withdrew her hand. "Where's my money?" When she saw Zack remove an envelope from the side pocket of his coat and hold it under the table, she snatched it.

"Don't worry. It's all there."

When she finished counting to verify the amount, she got up from the table without saying a word and left the café.

Regan O'Brien reclined in a swivel office chair behind his large mahogany desk in the O'Brien Import and Export Company, which he owned and operated. With his fingers interlaced while tapping his thumbs together, he waited patiently for the older of his two sons, Zack, to return with the list of artifacts being shipped to the Museum of Archeology and Anthropology.

Regan saw himself as the consummate businessman. He had the polish of a refined gentleman, with straight dark hair accentuated by a short pointed mustache and intense gray eyes. He invariably used his self-confident smile to gain and reinforce his legitimacy with each of his customers.

Regan knew that Zack's boldness often exceeded his best judgment. He also saw that Zack wanted to take charge of every situation but that he had little patience with those who disagreed with him.

On the other hand, Regan saw Alex, his younger son, as being less aggressive, but he also noticed that Alex had a logical mind capable of looking at situations more objectively than his brother did. Despite their differences, he saw that the bond between his sons remained strong and unbreakable.

Regan also had hired Jake Long and Hank Walker to do his dirty work. Since neither of them seemed to have any interest in artifacts, nor did they seem to see any real value in them, he knew that they only cared about being paid. They often worked alongside Regan's two sons, but Regan let Zack take charge. Regan relied heavily on the illegal aspects of his business to sustain the very comfortable lifestyle to which he had become accustomed.

When Zack finally arrived, Regan reviewed Laura's list and spotted a Ming vase that one of his customers had requested. "I'll need the Ming vase soon. It'll fetch a nice price from a customer I know in New York."

"It shouldn't ship to the museum until Monday at the earliest," Zack said. "Where's it located?"

"It's in warehouse number three at pier twenty-three."

"If you have the crate number, we can get it tonight. It's only about two hours before nightfall."

"It's in crate sixteen," Regan said. "You'll probably need to take Jake, Hank, and Alex along with you since the crate will be fairly large and will need careful handling."

The unmistakable smell of the sea filled the air around the Philadelphia dock area where multiple piers lined the shoreline. Seagulls perching on some of the taller pilings watched as silent sentinels of the activity on the wood-planked piers. Heavy mooring lines extended from the ships' capstans and then passed through line portals on the main decks to the large iron bollards on the piers. Multiple fore and aft lines snugly secured the ships in their individual berths. A seaman with a bulging seabag slung over his shoulder would occasionally climb a steep gangplank to a poorly lit quarterdeck and then disappear into one of the oblong-shaped doors in the superstructure.

The wooden and somewhat weathered warehouses stood opposite the piers. Each warehouse had a double door that faced the piers to allow the loading of crates to and from the ships. Single doors on each end of the warehouses allowed dock personnel inside to inspect and inventory the crates.

Zack told Hank to pull their wagon into a darkened alley several yards away from the pier. He then led Jake and Alex toward the warehouse, where they waited on the back side, away from the piers, until the security guard had checked the locks on this particular warehouse.

"We should have about twenty minutes before he returns," Zack said in a whisper. "It'll take him that long to check the locks on the warehouses of the adjacent piers." He then carefully moved around to the door on the side of the warehouse and quietly told Jake to cut the lock with a pair of bolt cutters he had brought. He removed the severed lock and opened the door, lighting a lantern hanging on the inside wall next to the door. After he entered, Jake followed him and Alex closed the door behind them.

Zack moved along the crates until he spotted the crate labeled "16," with the words *Ming Vase* below the number. "Here it is," Zack said. "Now I can see why all of us needed to come. It's going to take all of us to load it in the wagon. For now, we'll just have to slide it to the door."

"Look at this one!" Alex said. "It's a crate labeled seventeen, with the words *Healing Cup* below the number!"

"It does look interesting, but we only need the vase," Zack said.

"It's small enough for me to carry. Why not take it?"

Zack relented. "All right, but you'll have to help us with the big crate when we get to the wagon."

Zack and Jake began sliding the crate toward the door while Alex picked up the smaller crate and took the lantern. Zack and Jake finally reached the door after several hefty shoves of the large crate. Alex hung the lantern back on the wall and extinguished it.

Zack had started to push the door open when he heard a wagon pull up next to the dockside wall of the warehouse. "Hank was supposed to wait with the wagon until I signaled him," Zack said.

A tapping sound began on the wall facing the docks. The sound stopped and then started again after a few moments. It started again and then stopped again. It started one more time before stopping.

"It sounds like someone's hammering something on the wall," Alex said.

"We'll have to go out and check," Zack said. "We can't wait any longer. The guard might be coming back at any time."

Zack eased the door open and took a quick look around the corner of the warehouse. He saw a kid standing back from the wall as if admiring something he had just hung up. He ducked back around the corner and pondered what to do. He then saw Jake move quickly past him with his revolver raised. He flinched when the blast from the revolver nearly deafened him. When he looked toward the kid, he saw him crumpled in an awkward position on the ground. The scene stunned Zack for a moment, but he signaled Hank to bring their wagon up quickly next to the warehouse door. After the crates had been loaded and their wagon began to speed away, he looked back and saw a security guard sprinting toward the kid.

Regan's business sat on ground that sloped steeply to the rear of the business. As such, stairs inside the business led down to a main storage area. A hidden storage area under the upper level, where Regan sometimes temporarily kept his illegal acquisitions, could be accessed by sliding a large panel near the stairs.

Zack, Jake, and Hank unloaded the larger crate and lowered it onto the floor of the business's main storage area while Alex brought in the smaller crate and set it down on a nearby table.

"Why are there two crates?" Regan asked.

"I took the smaller crate because it looked interesting," Alex said. "It may not be anything we want, but the museum must have wanted it."

Regan examined the label. "It does look interesting, but you take unnecessary risks when you take more than you need to."

"Well, we did have a slight problem at the warehouse," Zack said.

Regan glared at Zack. "What do you mean by a 'slight problem'?"

"This kid showed up to nail something on the outside of the warehouse wall just when we were ready to leave," Zack said. "I had to shoot him so he wouldn't identify us."

Regan grimaced. "You what? Why didn't you just wait for the kid to leave?"

"We thought the security guard might be back at any minute," Zack said.

Regan put his hands on his hips. "This is the type of unnecessary risk I was talking about."

"We didn't know the kid was going to show up!" Zack said.

Regan gave Alex a stern look. "Perhaps if you hadn't spent time getting the other crate, you might have left before he got there."

"What should we do now?" Zack asked.

Regan sighed. "If we assume the kid is dead, we can lie low for a while."

"What if he's not dead?" Jake asked.

Regan bit his lower lip. "Then you'll have to take care of the problem, won't you?"

"Do you think you'll be able to sell the healing cup?" Alex asked.

Regan rubbed his chin for a moment. "Huh, I may know just the person who might buy it."

CHAPTER 11

GETTING ORGANIZED

Adam decided to have a meeting in John and Ann's kitchen before starting the investigations since he first wanted everyone get to know each other. He knew that having everyone going in a different direction could make the investigations even more difficult.

Adam didn't know how helpful Dan would be since he didn't have any field experience. He sensed that Dan might be a little impetuous and overconfident, but he hoped Dan could follow directions and become a meaningful member of the group. He could only hope that Dan's training in military school would be an asset, not a hindrance.

As for Merlin, he still saw him as somewhat of a mystery. He couldn't understand why Merlin seemed so intent on following the investigations. He wondered if Merlin's life had become so mundane that he needed some form of excitement. He had seen him show a lot of enthusiasm, but he didn't seem to be someone just looking for a thrill. His apparent teaching background seemed to indicate that he truly wanted to learn about investigations and, at the same time, be a helpful source of information.

Adam had invited Edward to join the meeting after he had finished unpacking his things in his room. He hoped that Edward had already talked with his supervisor about helping out in the investigations. He didn't think that Edward being a Lloyd's detective would be a handicap as far as his availability since most of the investigations would involve the theft of items that Lloyd's probably insured. He just knew it would be good to have Edward along because he trusted him since he remembered how well they had worked together on their assignments in graduate school. He only worried about Edward's apparent skepticism about almost everything. However, if reasonably used, he knew it could effectively sort out fact from fiction.

When Edward joined the meeting, Adam introduced Dan and Merlin. "Edward, I'd like you to meet Dan Covington. He's the son of Charles Covington, my supervisor. The other gentleman is Merlin Pendragon. He's just going to be a civilian observer who apparently has knowledge of many subjects. He may be a helpful source of information when we need him."

Adam watched Edward shake Dan's hand but saw him hesitate slightly when shaking Merlin's. He wondered what suspicions Edward might have about Merlin.

"You aren't that mythological wizard, Merlin, from the twelfth century, are you?" Edward asked.

"I dare say, old boy, that would make me into some sort of modern-day Methuselah, don't you think?"

Adam heard a knock on the side door to the kitchen and watched it slowly open. He hadn't expected anyone else at his meeting.

"Good morning, gentlemen. I hope I'm not intruding," Inspector Fagan said.

"Good morning, Inspector Fagan. I'd like you to meet Dan Covington, Charles Covington's son, and Merlin Pendragon, a civilian observer. I believe you already met Edward at the Broadmoor

Theater. We're all going to investigate the robberies at the Museum of Archeology and Anthropology."

"I'm pleased to meet each of you gentlemen. Please let me know if I can be of any assistance."

Adam saw Fagan eyeing a plate of bagels in the middle of the table. "Please have a seat, Inspector. There's always room for one more. Have a bagel and a cup of coffee."

"Why, thank you, Adam. I don't mind if I do. I just love bagels, you know. Would you mind passing the cream cheese?"

"What brings you here this early in the morning, Inspector?" Adam asked.

"I was hoping to find you here, Adam, because I didn't want to go all the way out to the circus just yet. I have some rather distressing news. A young boy was shot last night. He was hanging a circus poster on one of the warehouses down at the docks. I thought you might know who he is."

Adam showed concern. "Yes, I certainly might. I'd asked Uncle George to find some boys at the circus who would be interested in hanging up posters around the city. Can you tell me what happened? Is he all right?"

"Well, it seems he must have interrupted a robbery at the docks last night."

Adam covered one eye with his hand. "Oh God! Is he alive?"

"Barely. He's lost a lot of blood and is in critical condition. The doctors think he'll pull through because of his youth."

"It sounds like he's lucky to be alive," Edward said.

"Indeed," Fagan said. "He'd be dead if it hadn't been for the security guard and a doctor from a nearby ship."

Adam gave Fagan a concerned look. "The boy might be in danger if the shooter finds out he's still alive."

"I've already had an officer posted outside his door."

"I'm sorry, gentlemen, but I think I need to adjourn our meeting so I can go to the circus and see Uncle George," Adam said. "He'll need to notify the parents of the boy."

"I think we should all go to the circus with Adam," Merlin said. "I'm curious. I'd like to see it for myself."

"Very well. I have no objection," Adam said. "We can begin our investigations after the visit to the circus. Uncle George should be able to handle the situation with the boy and be sure he's going to be all right."

CHAPTER 12

THE SUSPECTS

Adam began their investigation at the port master's office. An elderly man with a sailor's hat cocked to one side on top of long gray hair sat behind a weathered oak desk. He had a face creased with age and covered with a stubbly beard. In the corner of his mouth, he gripped a pipe.

"May I help you, gentlemen?"

Adam displayed his badge. "We're investigating the shooting of a young boy at one of your warehouses."

"Ah, yes, indeed," the old man said. "I remember that evening. I do hope the poor lad's doing okay. I was told that he was about the age of my son."

"Can you tell us the warehouse where it occurred?" Edward asked.

"It was at warehouse three. It's quite a walk from here. I didn't see anything, but I did hear a gunshot. My son can unlock it for you."

"How is the transfer of the cargo made from the ship to the

warehouse?" Adam asked. He watched the old man take a puff on his pipe and then remove it from his mouth.

"Well, there're three documents involved in the transfer. The purser on the ship has the original bill of lading and two copies. As the cargo is unloaded onto wagons on the dock, he verifies the shipments against the original bill of lading. The purser then keeps one of the copies, and I get the rest. I select the warehouse and write the number on the original and the second copy. I keep the original and give the second copy to my son, who tells the dockworkers which warehouse to use. While the cargo is being loaded into the warehouse, I create an invoice for each item on the bill of lading, which my son will deliver to each recipient of a particular item."

"It sounds like you've got a good, workable system," Adam said.

"Well, it seems to work pretty well, but we do have occasional robberies like that one you're investigating. I just don't know how the robbers know what to take. Only me, my son, the purser, and the customer have the information."

"Can you tell us where we might find the purser's ship?" Adam asked.

"As a matter of fact, his ship's docked at pier twenty-three, right near the warehouse."

"Excellent," Adam said. "If your son can now take us to the warehouse, we'll interview the purser after we finish looking at the crime scene."

"Certainly. I'll go outside and call for him."

The warehouse didn't reveal anything suspicious either inside or outside. Adam stared at the circus poster on the side of the warehouse.

"Don't blame yourself," Merlin said. "There's no way you could have predicted what was going to happen to the boy."

Adam didn't say a word but dropped his head and brushed the ground with his foot as if trying to erase what had happened to the boy.

After questioning the purser, they stood at the end of the gangplank to the purser's ship.

"I don't think the dock master, his son, or the purser had anything to do with the theft," Edward said.

"I agree," Adam said. "They all seem to be honest people who work hard at their jobs. They don't seem to have the desire to jeopardize the lives they've created for themselves."

"Where do we go next?" Dan said.

"The Museum of Archeology and Anthropology," Adam said. "It's the only other place where the invoices were delivered."

"Maybe we'll find a suspicious-looking mummy, Dan!" Edward said.

Adam first saw Felix Franklin standing behind a semicircular marble reception desk inside the museum. Felix, an average-sized man, had narrow shoulders and a stiff posture. His pale, narrow face ended in a pointed chin, and his short hair had a distinct part on one side. Since he rarely smiled, Adam could only imagine him having the sense of humor of a rock.

Adam immediately noticed the large portrait and brass plate beneath it on the marble wall behind Felix, which seemed to extend upward forever. He saw similar facial characteristics between the man in the portrait and Felix. "I assume the man in the portrait behind you is your father?"

"Yes, it's a portrait of my late father. He built the museum from the ground up with the support of several wealthy donors, a multitude of patrons, and of course the city for its donation of the land. I'm very proud of it and of being its curator."

As curator of the Museum of Archaeology and Anthropology, his position allowed him to have total control of every aspect of the museum. Adam imagined that Felix also might treat his employees more like museum pieces than human beings. Had a disgruntled or former employee reviled at his control and decided to exact revenge on him?

"You just missed the eleven o'clock tour," Felix said. "The next one won't be until one o'clock."

"We're not here for the tour," Adam said. "We're investigating the theft of a Ming vase and a healing cup. We represent both the Pinkerton Detective Agency and the Lloyd's Insurance Company."

"Yes, the Ming vase," Felix said. "It was supposed to be one of our prized acquisitions."

"What about the healing cup?" Edward asked. "It sounds suspiciously like some kind of hoax."

"I don't disagree with you," Felix said. "It does sound incredible. I can't imagine anyone actually believing it could be like a Holy Grail, if not the Holy Grail itself. It was found on a small island off the coast of Wales. I thought we would acquire it purely as a curiosity for our museum guests. As you know, not everyone is enamored with looking at ancient artifacts. They need something to spice up, if you will, their visit."

"How are invoices handled?" Adam asked.

"I give the documents to Laura Morgan, my assistant. She records the items in a logbook and places the invoices in a pending folder."

"How are the items actually received?" Edward asked.

"Laura collects the invoices for the week and turns them over to the shipping and receiving department on each Friday for pickup on Monday."

"May we speak with Laura?" Adam asked.

"I don't want to interrupt her at this moment because she's in the middle of conducting the eleven o'clock tour."

"Have there been any thefts before this one?" Adam asked.

"There've been three or four in the past year, but there doesn't seem to be any pattern to what was taken."

"Was the same ship involved or were there different ships?" Adam asked.

"Oh, I'm almost sure it's never the same ship. We deal with shipments from all over the world."

"Do you have any reason to suspect anyone, such as a disgruntled or former employee?" Edward asked.

"I don't know about the former employees, but I treat all my current employees with the utmost respect. I haven't received a single complaint from any of them."

"Do you deal with any local antique dealers?" Edward asked.

"Mostly we deal with other museums, both nationally and internationally, but occasionally we purchase mundane items from the O'Brien Import and Export Company to liven up the interests of our visitors. By mundane, I mean items that don't really have any historical significance."

Adam saw a woman walk toward them from a group of people that started to mill about the main lobby. It appeared that their escorted tour had ended.

"Laura, I'd like you to meet these gentlemen from the Pinkerton Detective Agency and the Lloyd's Insurance Company," Felix said. "They're looking into the theft of the Ming vase and the healing cup."

"It's a pleasure, gentlemen."

"Laura is my only female employee, and I highly value her for the fine job she always does."

"Perhaps you gentlemen would like to take the one o'clock tour," Laura said. "I think you'd find it quite interesting."

"I think another time would be more appropriate," Adam said. "Our investigation takes priority right now. Thank you just the same."

"Then how may I help you, gentlemen?" Laura asked.

Adam noticed that Laura stood stiffly and held her hands tightly together in front her. He wondered what made her so uncomfortable. He hadn't even asked her a question yet. Was she afraid of something or did she have something to hide? "I assume you're the only one to receive the invoices from the docks."

"Yes, I collect them for the week and then give them to the shipping and receiving department. I spend the rest of my time conducting museum tours. It keeps me informed of what changes may have occurred in the displays."

"Does anyone besides you and the shipping and receiving department handle the documents?" Adam asked.

"Not that I'm aware of."

May we see your office?" Edward asked.

"Certainly. It's through a door behind this wall to your right."

"If you'll excuse me, gentlemen," Felix said, "I have some pressing matters of my own to attend to. Please let me know if you have any further questions."

"By the way, when do you expect your next shipment?" Merlin asked.

"Sometime next week."

Adam extended his hand. "Well, thank you very much, Felix. We'll contact you if we need any more information."

A cursory inspection of the office revealed nothing except Felix's immaculate and well-organized desk compared to Laura's somewhat disheveled desk. Adam began to speculate about how the information on the invoices had been stolen. Had an employee copied the information while Laura was giving a tour? Had a former employee who might still have a key to the museum entered after hours and copied the information? Had someone in the shipping and receiving department been the culprit? The possibility always existed that Laura herself had copied the information and had sold it to someone outside of the museum. He only remembered Laura's earlier nervousness. He then saw Merlin raise one finger questioningly. "Yes, Merlin. Do you have a question?"

"Not at the moment, but I think I'd like to take one of those tours of the museum while the rest of you go ahead. I'm anxious to see anything that I might not have seen before. Besides, I'd also like to talk with Felix some more when he's available."

"Feel free, Merlin. Your time is your own. We'll meet up with you tomorrow. In the meantime, I was going to suggest that we all go have something to eat. You're welcome to come if you want to put off the tour."

"No, I think I'll stay here, but thank you for the invitation."

"I don't know about the rest of you, but I'm starving," Dan said.

Adam and rest of his intrepid group arrived the next day at the O'Brien Import and Export Company on the edge of the city. A waist-high stone wall guarded the grounds to the front entrance of a redbrick building having pairs of windows on either side of a white wooden door. A medium-sized sign with the Company's name hung below the apex of the roof.

As soon as they entered, Adam saw Regan O'Brien stand up next to his desk. To his right, he saw Regan's two sons, Zack and Alex, sitting at a table near one of the windows while playing checkers. A curtain to the right of the desk stretched across a doorway. Adam suspected that the doorway led to a large storage area.

"Good afternoon, gentlemen. My name's Regan O'Brien. How may I help you?"

Adam showed his badge. "We're here to investigate the theft of a Ming vase and a healing cup."

"Yes, I read about that dreadful incident in the newspaper, but I don't deal in antiquities."

"Why is that?" Edward asked.

"Well, you see, all countries protect their antiquities and don't allow them to be sold or transported out of their borders. The one exception is for museums to loan artifacts to each other for a limited time for display purposes only."

"You seem to know quite a bit about antiquities," Edward said.

"Not as much as you might think. However, I did major in archaeology in college, but I just couldn't see digging in the dirt all my life."

"Have you heard any rumors about other thefts of antiquities?" Adam asked.

"I'm much too busy to pay attention to rumors. Besides, I usually don't believe them anyway."

Adam shook Regan's hand. "Well, thank you very much for your time, Mister O'Brien. Please let the Pinkerton Detective Agency or the Lloyd's Insurance Company know if you hear anything about the Ming vase or healing cup thefts."

"Certainly, gentlemen."

After the guests left, Regan put his hands on his hips. "Zack! Alex! Get over here! Did the two of you overhear my conversation with those detectives?"

"Yeah, but I don't know what brought them here," Zack said.

Regan pursed his lips. "It was probably Felix Franklin at the museum." He saw Jake and Hank push the curtain aside and enter the room.

"What's going on?" Jake asked.

Regan gave Jake a stern look. "We had a visit from some Pinkerton and Lloyd's detectives."

"Do you want us to take care of them?"

Regan sighed. "No, it's too risky, and it might attract too much attention. However, there's something you can do to keep them from getting any closer."

"Yeah, what's that?"

"I read in the paper that the boy you shot is recovering in the Pennsylvania Hospital."

"I knew I should've made sure he was dead," Jake said.

"Well, now's your chance to finish the job. This time don't make any more mistakes."

"We know what to do."

CHAPTER 13

A CLOSE CALL

Merlin relaxed in the cushioned chair in his room at the bookstore and stared out of the window while Gwen slowly rocked in her rocking chair with an open book against her chest. He thought that the investigation had started rather well. From his viewpoint, none of the interviews seemed to point to any particular individual. This didn't deter him, for he now realized that investigations, though tedious, tended to eliminate those things that didn't seem possible or definitive, leaving the more probable aspects of the crime to ponder. During his separate meeting with Felix, his mind began to speculate about a possible solution concerning the thefts. Of course, he'd need Felix's help and he'd have to first present it to the rest of the group to get their concurrence.

"How'd the investigation go today?" Gwen asked. "Did you make any progress?"

"Some. We mostly conducted interviews."

"Ann and I had some lovely discussions over tea," Gwen said.

"She seemed glad to have another female in the bookstore to talk to. However, I was careful to keep our secrets about our identities and time traveling. I felt bad about deceiving her, but there wasn't any choice."

"You did the right thing, Gwen. The people in this century are not prepared to accept who we truly are or how we got here."

"I realize that the best thing we can do is to blend in," Gwen said. "We could never go back to the twelfth century. I wouldn't be comfortable knowing what the future was like."

Suddenly, Merlin began to tremble with a blank stare in his eyes.

"Are you seeing another vision, Merlin?"

A few moments later, Merlin returned to normal. He shook his head several times and then rubbed his eyes.

"What did you see this time?" Gwen asked.

"I saw two men. They approached a hospital room. I saw a young boy in the room before they opened the door. Oh my God, it might be the boy from the circus who was shot the other evening! They must not want the boy to identify them. They're going to kill him!"

"Is there anything you can do?"

"I'll try to communicate with Adam again." With that said, Merlin went into another trance.

That same day, Adam and Edward met for an early dinner at the Upton Café on Cumberland Street. Adam picked at a Waldorf salad as he gazed out of the café window while Edward gorged himself on a Philly cheesesteak sandwich.

"What's bothering you, old chap?"

"I'm just trying to put the pieces of this case together."

"Don't worry. You will. We could have less to work with, you know."

Adam suddenly dropped his fork on the edge of his salad bowl. A loud clatter shattered the silence.

"Adam, what is it?"

Adam didn't respond but stared into empty space.

"Adam, speak to me. What's wrong?"

Adam shook his head as he came back to normal. He turned his face toward Edward. "Did you say something?"

"No, but what happened? You gave me a scare. Are you all right?"

Adam nodded. "Yes, but I had another one of those strange feelings that someone was speaking to me."

"That again? We have to get you some help, old chap. It's just not normal for you to be hearing voices in your head."

Adam pleaded. "I'm serious! We've got to leave right now!"

"Why? What did this voice tell you?"

Adam removed his napkin and turned in his chair. "The voice said that two men are going to approach a hospital room. There's a boy in the room. I think it might be the circus boy. They're going to kill him!"

Adam and Edward ran into the hospital and darted to the hallway. Two men approached the police officer at the door to the boy's room.

Adam shouted, "Stop!"

The two men turned in the direction of the voice and drew their revolvers. The guard also appeared startled but didn't seem sure what to do.

Adam ducked back around the corner of the entrance to the hallway when Jake fired a shot at him. Instinctively and without reservation, he dove to the hallway floor and returned fire. His shot hit Jake in the chest. He watched Jake crumple to the floor. He then saw Hank turn toward the police officer when Hank sensed the officer's movement. He started to take a shot at Hank but feared he might hit the officer. He looked toward Edward because he thought Edward might have a better angle. A moment later, Edward fired a shot and Hank slumped to the floor as well.

The boy cautiously peeked out of the door to his hospital room. "He's the one! He's the one who shot me!"

"It looks like you got your man," Edward said.

Adam wiped his brow. "In another minute, we would've been too late."

Edward sighed. "I still think your premonitions are getting stranger."

"Nonetheless, it saved the boy's life, didn't it?"

"I know, but this is still too hard for anyone to believe."

Adam's voice stammered. "I … I may have an answer that you as well may not believe."

Edward crossed his arms. "I'm all ears."

"I visited Madame Gisele, the fortune-teller at the circus, the other day."

"Really! What irrefutable advice did she give you?"

"Believe it or not, she actually contacted someone or something through her crystal ball."

"Rubbish! Don't you realize that you've just been deceived by one of her parlor tricks? No one has ever been able to communicate with another individual by only using their mind!"

"But it's true. I swear! We both saw the distorted face of a man in the crystal ball."

"I don't believe any of this. Did this vision actually speak?"

"No, the connection was too much for her. She had to break it off."

"I'm not surprised. You know, you really need to get some professional help for your own sanity, Adam."

CHAPTER 14

A SHADY DEAL

Regan felt confident that he knew the perfect person to con into buying the healing cup. The whole absurd notion that a healing cup could actually heal someone didn't matter. He just knew that his job of selling the healing cup became easier by preying on the desperation of the person that thought they could be healed by it. He couldn't understand why a reputable museum like the Museum of Archeology and Anthropology had ever considered obtaining such a ridiculous item. Nonetheless, he now had the healing cup, and he saw an excellent opportunity to make a reasonable profit with minimal effort.

Regan approached the house of Owen Parks, an editor at the *Philadelphia Inquirer.* He and Owen had a long-term adversarial relationship since Owen had blackmailed him for years over a note from John Wilkes Booth that implicated him in the Lincoln assassination. He didn't see any way to avoid paying Owen if he wanted to avoid the hangman's noose. If he tried to get rid of Owen, the note might reach the authorities by whatever means Owen had set up. He couldn't take a chance unless he could no longer trust Owen to keep his secret.

He climbed the steps to a broad porch that extended the full width of a single-story white clapboard house. On the right side of the porch, a swing hung from hooks in the porch ceiling. On the left side, a small round table had been positioned between two rocking chairs. He opened a screen door and knocked on a light brown stained door with a small window near the top.

After waiting for a few moments, Eva Sims, Owen's niece, opened the door.

"May I see Rita Sims?" Regan asked. "Rita and I are old friends."

"Certainly. Come right this way."

Regan followed Eva into the sitting room, where Rita, Eva's mother, sat in her wheelchair by the fireplace. He noticed that she looked thinner than he remembered, with a face somewhat withered from age. He thought that she probably suffered from depression about her lack of mobility.

"Regan, it's been a long time since we've seen each other. Please have a seat."

"How have you been, Rita?"

"About as well as can be expected. It seems like an eternity since the accident."

The accident immediately prompted Regan's memory of Rita recounting her life in Richmond to him. To begin with, her husband, a Confederate officer, protected the Richmond railroad depot near the end of the Civil War. When the siege of Richmond became more intense, she planned to take a train out of the city before it fell. However, when the Union blockaded the rail lines, she had no choice but to travel by carriage to Philadelphia with her slave, Ezra, to live with her sister, Quinta. Before she left, she saw her husband burn the train she had planned to take. She couldn't understand why the train needed to be burned since she saw a seemingly countless number of bags being loaded into an unusual compartment in the floor of the caboose. She asked him about the compartment and the bags, but he told her that he thought it would be too dangerous for her to know. Then the unimaginable happened when she saw her husband killed by a Union bombardment.

Regan then remembered when he had seen Rita in Washington and had told her that the war had ended. The irony of her husband's death so close to the war's end had left her in despair. Unknowingly, she became involved in a conspiracy with Regan and his friend, John Wilkes Booth, to assassinate President Lincoln. She only had to fake a fainting spell to draw a guard away from the stairs to the second-floor balcony at Ford's Theatre where President Lincoln sat. In their escape, she watched Regan stab a police officer before they took a perilous carriage ride through the city. When the carriage turned over, her legs became pinned under the carriage. Since then, she hadn't been able to walk.

Regan eased into a chair near Rita's wheelchair. "It does to me too, but I came to see if you had read the newspaper article about the robbery at the docks."

"Yes, but it didn't seem very important to me."

"You may have noticed that the article mentioned a healing cup had also been stolen."

"That sounds like a hoax to steal someone's money."

"It may not be. The museum was going to put it on display as a genuine artifact. Who knows—maybe it has some mythical power. You'd like to walk again, wouldn't you?"

"You can't be serious, Regan. Do you really think it's possible?"

"Isn't it worth trying? I know how to obtain it for the right price."

Regan saw Quinta, Rita's sister and Owen's wife, start down the stairs from her bedroom. He instantly noticed her svelte body and slender legs.

"You'd be foolish to consider buying a fancy cup that's probably worth nothing," Quinta said.

"You're not the one in the wheelchair," Rita said.

"He's probably the one who stole the cup so he can make a profit by selling it to you."

"It doesn't matter to me who stole it or why," Rita said. "How much do you want for it, Regan?"

"As a museum piece, it's probably worth about fifteen thousand dollars."

"That's absurd!"

"As a friend, I could give it to you for ten thousand dollars."

"Let me think about it. I'll have to figure out how to get the money."

Regan saw Quinta throw up her hands. He hoped her action wouldn't sway Rita away from the potential deal.

"This is the most ridiculous thing you've ever thought about doing, Rita!" Quinta said.

"Let me know what you want to do," Regan said.

"Wait a minute, Regan," Rita said. "Do you know of anyone who could loan me the money?"

"I do know of someone who might be able to help you. I'll contact him if you'd like me to. His name's Vance Watts."

"Thank you, Regan. I'll be looking forward to meeting with him."

The next day, Vance Watts knocked on the door. A giant of a man stood behind him. Vance smiled broadly. "We'd like to see Rita Sims. My name's Vance Watts."

"Certainly. I think she's been expecting you," Eva said.

Vance and Titus Urban, his enormous companion, entered the sitting room and found Rita in her wheelchair by the fireplace. "I'm Vance Watts, and my friend's Titus Urban. Regan O'Brien thought we might be of assistance to you."

"Yes, I certainly hope so. Please have a seat."

Vance scanned the room as if making a mental inventory of its contents. His mind began to assess the wealth of the occupant in the room. "How much do you need to borrow?"

"I'll need ten thousand dollars."

"Whew, that's a tidy sum!"

"I need it for a healing cup Regan said he could get for me."

"I assume it has something to do with your being in a wheelchair."

"I want to walk again!"

Vance raised an eyebrow. "You're really serious about this healing cup, aren't you?"

"I'm willing to try anything to be able to walk again."

Vance rubbed his chin. "I couldn't loan you that much money, but there may be another way. Are you really willing to try anything?"

"What do you mean?"

Vance bent close to Rita and whispered, "We could make the money ourselves."

"You mean actually make counterfeit money?"

Vance smirked. "Regan wouldn't know the difference."

"Your plan sounds preposterous!"

Vance put his finger to his lips. "Not really. In fact, my source tells me that a counterfeiter is due to be released from prison in a few days."

"What's in it for you?" Rita asked.

"Well, I thought he could make some cash for me while he was at it."

"But counterfeiting is a major crime. What are our chances of getting caught?"

Vance pursed his lips. "There's very little with the right engraving plates, ink, and paper."

"Assuming I go along with this plan, how would you go about it?"

Vance sat back in his chair. "First of all, I need some place that's discreet and unused."

"There's a carriage house in back of the house that's partially unused since we no longer have any permanent household help. One side's just for Owen's carriage and his horse."

"Excellent. That'll give us a place to make the money. Titus and I will need to kidnap the counterfeiter and hold him hostage there."

"All this sordid counterfeiting and kidnapping is making me nervous."

Vance squinted with one eye. "How badly did you say you wanted to walk again?"

"All right, you've made your point. What do you need to do next?"

"Well, after we kidnap the counterfeiter, Titus and I will convince him to show us where to find the printing press and engraving plates that he used before he was arrested."

"What about the ink and paper?"

"We'll also convince him to show us where to find those things too."

"You seem pretty sure of yourself. What makes you think this is really going to work?"

Vance rubbed his cheeks. "I've thought about this many times. All I needed was the counterfeiter to be released from prison."

"Okay, what do you need from me?"

"Just give me your spare keys to the carriage house."

"By the way, I don't want Owen, my brother-in-law, to know what's going on," Rita said. "He usually leaves early in the morning, and I don't usually see him until dinnertime. If he does see you, tell him that you and Titus are old friends of mine from Richmond and that I'm temporarily letting you use the left side of the carriage house until you find a permanent place to stay."

CHAPTER 15
THE PLAN

Adam held a second meeting in John and Ann's kitchen to formulate a plan of action concerning the thefts at the museum. So far, the investigation contained only bits and pieces of information from key interviews. Nothing had yet enticed him to move ahead in a particular direction.

For someone to know when a particular artifact had reached the docks, they'd have to review the bills of lading or the invoices every day. The elderly dock master and his young son certainly didn't give the appearance of being involved. The ship's purser could be involved with someone onshore, but the purser on every ship would have to be involved since the museum items could be transported on different ships. That scenario seemed highly unlikely. The only suspects left would have to be either former museum employees or individuals at the museum.

"Does anyone have a suggestion on how to proceed with the investigation?" Adam asked.

"I have one main concern," Edward said. "Since the thieves are selective as to which artifacts they want to steal, it may take weeks or even months to catch them in the act."

"I think I can help with that concern," Merlin said. "I've had discussions with Felix about the next anticipated shipment to the museum. It's a valuable shipment of a seven-inch solid gold figurine of the Egyptian deity Amun-Re from the Museum of Cairo. What thief could possibly resist such a temptation?"

"I think you're right, Merlin," Adam said. "What's your plan?"

"We need to coordinate with the dock master to have his son notify us as soon as possible about the figurine's arrival and its warehouse location. We can then monitor the theft at the warehouse as it happens and follow the thieves to wherever they take the figurine."

"There's something else we need to do before the theft," Edward said.

"What's that, Edward?" Adam asked.

"I think we also still need to determine how the thieves get the warehouse information. Even after we capture the thieves, the informant could find other thieves to sell the warehouse information to."

"That also still concerns me, Edward," Adam said. "Of all the witnesses that we've interviewed, Laura's nervousness during her interview still puzzles me. I think we need to start with her."

"We need someone to follow her next Friday to see who she may make contact with and what she may do at the meeting," Merlin said.

"Why Friday?" Dan asked.

"Because that gives the thieves the weekend to get the artifact before the museum tries to pick it up on the coming Monday," Edward said.

"I'd like to be the person to follow her," Dan said. "I have excellent training in making observations. Can I wear a disguise?"

"That won't be necessary," Adam said. "Just blend in as best as you can at a safe distance to avoid detection. Be careful, though, and don't take any unnecessary chances. We still don't know who we're dealing with."

"I understand."

After Merlin and Dan left the kitchen, Adam thought about how Charles had trusted him to look after Dan. He then thought about his failed promise to look after Tim. Had he made a mistake by letting Dan follow Laura? But what else could he do? Since Laura had seen all of them, the nearby presence of him and the others would only give Dan away.

"Don't worry. It's a bloody good plan, old chap," Edward said.

Adam furrowed his brow. "I hope so."

CHAPTER 16

THE TRANSACTION

Vance's counterfeiting scheme didn't seem to have any flaws, but he did have concerns about the counterfeiter being uncooperative. He needed some leverage, but he couldn't take a chance on Titus hurting him too severely. An alternate plan hatched in his brain when he decided to follow the counterfeiter to his girlfriend's house just after he had been released from the Eastern State Penitentiary. He didn't interfere with their happy reunion but waited for the counterfeiter to be alone before attempting to kidnap him. He knew their separation would create the desired anxiety in both of them, particularly in the counterfeiter by threatening to harm his girlfriend.

The kidnapping went smoothly and without notice by anyone. He now had the leverage of the girlfriend's safety, and he easily coerced his victim into revealing the location of the counterfeiting equipment he had left stored away before being arrested. After collecting all the necessary equipment, which included the printing press, engraving plates, ink, a cutting board, and the paper used by the government, he proceeded in setting up a counterfeiting shop in the left side of Rita's carriage house.

He knew the terrified concern for the girlfriend would prompt the counterfeiter to produce the required amount of fake money, plus some for himself, in a matter of days. When his prediction came true, he didn't hesitate to take Rita's portion of the fake money to Regan and return with the healing cup.

"How could you tell the fake money from real money?" Rita asked. "Do you think Regan suspected anything?"

"The serial numbers for each denomination are same. The casual observer would never notice."

"I assume you had some made for yourself."

Vance smiled. "I've taken care of my needs for quite some time."

"By the way, I want you to move that equipment back to where you got it from and to release our guest away from here."

"Don't worry," Vance said. "He won't have a clue as to where he's been. We kept him blindfolded the whole time, except when he was in the carriage house."

"I hope you're right. This whole thing could come back on both of us, you know. I don't relish the thought of going to jail."

"I don't either, but here's your healing cup." After taking a small box from Titus, he watched Rita open the box with eager anticipation.

The cup radiated a golden brilliance accentuated by small diamonds, rubies, emeralds, and sapphires. The inscription on the side had a mythical quality: GIVE THINE SELF THE ELIXIR OF LIFE AND BE RENEWED.

"It's quite remarkable, don't you think?" Vance said. "The jewels themselves could fetch a fair price."

"I'm not interested in its material value but in its magic and what it can do for me. Do you think it could be the Holy Grail?"

Vance scoffed at the comment. "I doubt it. That's just a myth, you know."

"I take it that you're not a religious man."

"Let's just say that I'm a skeptic. Religion has never put food on my plate. I survive by what comes my way and by what it takes to get it."

"I'm not as cynical as you are," Rita said. "I believe in miracles. This chalice will be a test of my faith."

"Then let's put it to the test."

"Very well," Rita said. "Put some water in the cup and bring it back to me, Eva."

"I do sincerely hope it works for you, Mother."

"We'll see, dear."

Vance watched Rita take a sip and extended his lower lip as if showing confidence in his skepticism.

"I still can't move them!"

"Perhaps we should try some wine," Eva said.

"Yes, dear, perhaps you're right. Go put some wine in the cup."

"Let's hope this works."

Vance watched Rita take another sip.

"Nothing—absolutely nothing! Get this worthless thing out of my sight!" Rita threw the cup against the fireplace hearth.

Vance picked it up. "I'm amazed that it doesn't show the least bit of damage. Do you want me to sell it?"

"No, give it to Eva. She can put it in a prominent place in my bedroom as a reminder to never be so foolish again."

"What's going to happen if Regan finds out that the money is counterfeit?" Eva asked.

"It doesn't matter. As far as I'm concerned, since he got fake money and I got a fake cup, we're even."

CHAPTER 17

THE STAKEOUT

Dan Covington sat at an outdoor table in front of a coffee shop across the street from the entrance to the Museum of Archaeology and Anthropology. He had trouble containing himself and unconsciously shook one leg vigorously up and down. He couldn't believe he would soon begin his first solo assignment as a Pinkerton detective. He wanted it to be perfect, and he could hardly wait another minute for it to start.

At a few minutes after five o'clock on this particular Friday, the museum employees began streaming out of the museum's front door. He had no difficulty in picking out Laura Morgan from the other male employees. He saw that she walked with a determined stride while ignoring everyone else. He also saw that her shorter height didn't impede her speed since she walked faster to keep up with the pack.

After she turned left, he waited until she had walked about half a block before he stood up and began walking on his side of the street in the same direction. His nonchalant swagger drew more attention than it should have since his attempts to be inconspicuous by pulling his hat down over his eyes often resulted in his running into bystanders. In spite of his ineptness, he did manage to follow Laura for three blocks, until she stopped and entered the Bellevue Café. He then dashed across the street and walked briskly to the café's front door but didn't enter.

He waited a minute or so outside of the café to be sure Laura had been seated. He then entered and sat down at a table on the far side of the dining room. He took off his hat, picked up the menu, and pretended to be studying it. With a casual glance over the top of his menu, he saw Laura seated at a table with a man he instantly recognized. He remembered the man being one of the two men sitting at a table in the O'Brien Import and Export Company.

Laura sat awkwardly in her chair and looked past Zack with a nervous glance about the room.

"What's wrong, Laura? You seem upset today," Zack said.

"It's that man at the table on the far side of the room. He followed me here."

"So? What's wrong with a man following an attractive woman like you? I have the exact same affliction he does."

"It's not what you think. He's one of the detectives who visited the museum the other day."

"Don't worry about him. Do you have the list?"

"Of course, but this is the last time. I don't like being followed."

Laura slid a piece of paper across the table to the man, and the man passed an envelope under the table.

"There's no reason to be hasty, Laura. Perhaps we could find another discreet rendezvous."

"I don't think so. Those detectives are too close for my comfort."

"What a shame. I'll sorely miss our little encounters."

"Speak for yourself," Laura said. "I hope I never see you again."

Dan watched Laura leave and then saw the man get up and casually walk past him with a limp in his right leg. His assignment seemed to have actually ended before it really began, but he had observed what he needed to see. It became obvious that Laura had to be the one who leaked the warehouse information for money to one of the two men at the O'Brien Import and Export Company. This, of course, assumed that the transaction actually involved the warehouse information and not something else since he didn't have a chance see what the note contained. Yet everything he saw seemed to make sense. It had to be the warehouse information. Why else would Laura briefly meet the man immediately after leaving the museum on a Friday and give him a note?

Meanwhile, Adam received the warehouse information for the Egyptian figurine from the dock master's son at the bookstore. He now realized that the next phase of Merlin's plan loomed ahead. If the figurine truly appealed to the thieves' greed, tonight had to be the night when he, Edward, and Merlin would watch the warehouse break-in. Depending on where the thieves took the figurine, he might find out where other stolen antiquities were located and possibly if a mastermind behind the thefts existed.

CHAPTER 18

THE THEFT

Adam pulled their wagon into a nearby alleyway not far from the rear of warehouse number nine, which stood opposite pier twenty-nine. Earlier in the evening, he had identified the location of warehouse nine by the large white number above the front double doors. As the evening progressed, the absence of moonlight from a new moon effectively hid practically everything and made his night vision struggle to make out the smaller details. With stealth, he and Edward took advantage of the darkness to leave the wagon with Merlin and move closer to the warehouse. The continued quiet around the warehouse made Adam think that the thieves hadn't yet arrived. He did eventually make out the shape of a security guard who made a sight metallic sound when he pulled on the warehouse padlocks.

Several hours passed before they heard wagon movement and the sound of horse hooves. Adam tensed and strained to determine the direction of the sound. He saw a wagon turn away from the piers and move around to the back of the warehouse. Nothing happened for some time, until he again heard the security guard checking the padlocks.

"They must have waited for the security guard to make his round so he would be gone for a while," Adam whispered.

"I think you're right, Adam. Let's see what happens next."

Two men appeared at the side door and stood next to it for a moment as if pondering their next move. Adam heard a dull snap like a twig breaking.

"They must have cut the padlock with something," Adam whispered again.

"They won't be here much longer after they find the crate with the figurine in it," Edward said.

When the side door opened with an audible creak, the two men disappeared inside and slowly closed the door behind them with another creak. A sliver of light beneath the door indicated that they had lit a lantern. A few minutes passed before the light disappeared and the door reopened.

"They must have found the artifact," Adam said. "Let's quickly get back to our wagon so we can follow before we lose sight of them."

The two men in their wagon didn't seem to realize that Adam's wagon followed a safe distance behind to avoid detection. The trip itself didn't last terribly long, but Adam had to remain alert to follow the wagon through several turns in the city. At one point, he nearly lost the wagon in the Meadowlawn Cemetery, which covered the equivalent of several city blocks. Unpredictably, the wagon with the two men had taken a path through the cemetery, where it seemed to disappear among the multiple tombs and mausoleums. A slight breeze chilled Adam's spine, as if the departed had all exhaled at the same time. A moment later, when he had the sense of a bony hand about to grasp his shoulder, his whole body shivered. The paths seemed to go on without end, until he heard Merlin break the silence.

"There it is!" Merlin said. "Take your next right. That should put you behind it again."

"Thanks, Merlin," Adam said. "I'd totally lost sight of it."

"I'm just as glad that we got out of the cemetery," Edward said. "This place is bloody creepy at night."

The rest of the trip didn't have any more unforeseen detours but began to look familiar to Adam. Then it became clear. They were heading along the same path they had taken to the O'Brien Import and Export Company. Adam soon pulled their wagon to a stop a short distance from the company building.

"Why are we stopping?" Merlin asked. "We should go inside and arrest those blokes right away and find the figurine. The thieves are obviously the O'Briens."

"It's not that simple, Merlin," Adam said. "We can't search the O'Brien Import and Export Company premises without the owner's permission, and I doubt they're going to give it."

"Rubbish! That's absurd!"

"That's the law, Merlin," Edward said. "We'll need Inspector Fagan to get a search warrant after he convinces a judge of probable cause."

"Since I can't do anything about the warrant, I'd like to focus on the O'Briens," Merlin said. "I now suspect we can assume that the O'Briens must also have been involved in the theft of the Ming vase and the healing cup as well."

"That would make sense since they may have received the warehouse information from the same person," Adam said. "We should be able to verify that when Dan tells us whom Laura met with. My guess would be one of the O'Brien brothers."

"What about Regan O'Brien?" Edward asked. "To me, this means that he's the mastermind of this whole operation. He also must have hired those men we killed at the hospital."

"I couldn't agree more, Edward," Adam said. "We now just have to prove it. The key will be finding the artifacts in the possession of the O'Briens."

"Once we get the search warrant, we can make a surprise visit," Merlin said. "It'll be bloody good to catch them with their knickers in a twist."

Inside the O'Brien Import and Export Company's main storage

area, Regan eagerly pried open the small crate without hesitation. He found the figurine's brilliant gold surface breathtaking. He instantly knew he had to have it in his own personal collection.

"You don't look like you want to sell it," Zack said.

"Certainly not, son. Can you imagine a solid gold figurine of an Egyptian god? I don't think I've ever seen anything quite like it before. It could worth a fortune."

"Then why not sell it?" Alex asked.

"Because I'm awed by its sheer beauty and magnificence. I'll have a place of prominence for it in my collection."

"Then you're taking it with you?" Alex asked.

"Yes, of course. Wrap it up and store the empty crate in the hidden storage area—but first paint over the information on the crate."

CHAPTER 19

THE SEARCH

Late the next day, two carriages arrived at the O'Brien Import and Export Company. Adam had Edward, Dan, and Merlin in one carriage, and Inspector Fagan had two police officers in another carriage. It seemed like a normal day at the business. With no other carriages in front of the business, it appeared that no customers remained inside. Through the far right window, two men could be seen sitting at a small table. Besides that, nothing else appeared noteworthy.

Earlier, Adam had thanked Inspector Fagan for getting the search warrant because he knew that it probably had consumed the better part of a day. He waited with the others in his group behind Fagan and the two policemen as Fagan rapped on the door. He watched Regan open the door with his usual gleeful smile but noticed that Regan looked more surprised than anything.

"Inspector, how nice to see you. Come right in. How may I help you?"

"I'm here on official business, O'Brien," Fagan said. "I'm here to serve a search warrant of these premises."

"Whatever for, Inspector? I don't understand."

Adam watched Fagan hand the search warrant to Regan as the two officers split up to begin the search. Regan unfolded the document and begin consuming its contents.

"There must be some mistake, Inspector. I don't know anything about a figurine."

"Two men in a wagon were followed here from a warehouse at the docks the other night. These detectives observed the break-in of the warehouse and the removal of a small crate. Would you know anything about that?"

"Certainly not, Inspector. I run a legitimate business here. We close the business well before it gets dark. The wagon must have stopped at some other place."

"Well, if you have nothing to hide, this search will be nothing but a formality. If nothing is found, we'll excuse ourselves and apologize for the intrusion."

"Be my guest, Inspector. We have nothing to hide."

The two officers had to go down at least a dozen steps to reach the main storage area. Adam guessed the height of the upper level to be about ten feet above the main storage area. He didn't consider this unusual since the outside land sloped dramatically from the front of the building. To make both levels the same elevation would require the main storage area to be on tall pilings.

He watched Merlin with interest as he examined the forward wall of the main storage area near the stairs. He suspected that Merlin might have found something since he occasionally tapped on the wall at different locations.

"What are you looking for, Merlin?" Adam asked. "Do you think there's something behind the wall?"

"I'm hearing a hollow sound at certain places. I think there may be an open area somewhere behind the wall. I just haven't found a way to open it."

"The only features on the wall are two wooden strips that run

84

the full height of the wall. Maybe they'll somehow allow us to open the wall."

"Give me a hand, Adam. Let's see if we can move them."

Adam helped Merlin pull on the strips. Surprisingly, the wall slid easily toward the stairs when they pulled on the one farthest from the stairs. Adam picked up a small open crate near the opening and examined the outside of it.

"It looks like the size of the crate that the figurine would be shipped in," Merlin said.

"Indeed it does, but it looks like someone has painted over the shipping information," Adam said. He then heard someone's shoes clopping down the stairs. He guessed that it might be Regan.

"That's just a spare storage area in case we have an overflow of items," Regan said. "As for that crate, we found it alongside the road. Since we didn't have an immediate use for it, I had it put in here so it didn't get mixed in with anything else."

"This additional storage area is certainly well hidden," Adam said.

"It surprised me as well when I found it," Regan said. "The previous owner of the building must have had some purpose for making it that way. Who knows? Maybe it was something clandestine."

Adam watched Fagan approach with his hands spread apart as if trying to indicate that nothing had been found. He sensed that the police officers had completed their search.

"I think you're in the clear, O'Brien, except I see there's something in this new opening in the wall that looks like the crate in question."

"As I explained to these gentlemen, it was found along the road and placed here in this overflow area to temporarily get it out of the way."

"Very well, then," Fagan said. "If these gentlemen are satisfied, we'll be leaving now. Please accept our apology for the intrusion."

Adam huddled with everyone outside the O'Brien business, near the carriages. He couldn't understand how they missed finding the figurine. The small crate certainly seemed incriminating. But what had they done with the figurine?

"What'd you think, Merlin?" Adam asked.

"I think he's a bona fide bloody liar. He knew that crate was the one we were looking for. I don't believe a word about that overflow storage area either. He's as slimy as they come."

"I think I agree with Merlin," Edward said. "We're at a dead end."

"There's always the house where he lives," Dan said.

"That may be, but I don't think there's sufficient probable cause to get another search warrant at this time," Fagan said. "Bring me some substantial evidence and then we'll see."

"Maybe you could have someone keep an eye on his place," Adam said. "It might turn up something."

"I suppose I could do that," Fagan said. "There're probably foot patrolmen who routinely watch over that area anyway. I can have them report anything suspicious."

CHAPTER 20

COUNTERFEIT MONEY

The Hargrove Bank didn't have a grandiose lobby like the larger banks in Philadelphia, but it survived the competition by offering more personalized service to its customers. Upon entering the bank, customers faced only two teller windows in the center of the lobby. Against the left wall, two stand-up tables provided customers a place to fill out their transaction information. A low wooden railing on the right guarded the bank manager's desk, and a large vault door consumed the back wall.

Owen Parks entered the lobby and immediately walked over to Eva's teller window. He pulled out an overstuffed envelope from his coat's vest pocket.

"Good morning, Eva."

"Good morning, Uncle Owen."

"I'd like to make a deposit to my account." He watched Eva take the envelope and begin counting the bills. Eva then did something curious—she carefully laid out the bills in a parallel arrangement. "Why are you doing that, Eva? Is there something wrong?"

"It's just a precaution, Uncle Owen. We've been notified that there's been some counterfeiting lately in the city."

"I certainly hope there's nothing wrong with these bills. I just received them from an associate of mine." It never dawned on him that the blackmail money he had received from Regan might be counterfeit. Surely Regan had to be smarter than this.

Eva looked up at him with a shocked stare. "Uncle Owen, they're not real!"

"That can't be! How can you tell?"

"The serial numbers are the same on bills of the same denomination!"

Owen's rage began to build. How could a scoundrel like Regan think he could get away with this? "Give me back the money, Eva. I'll take care of this myself."

"But, Uncle Owen, I'm supposed to report this!"

"Never mind that," Owen whispered. "Just forget you ever saw it. It's now my problem to solve. Do you understand?"

Owen rushed home from the bank without a moment's hesitation. Outrage replaced logic when he yanked open his desk drawer and removed his Colt revolver. When he arrived at Regan's wood-frame house, he took bold strides up to the front door. He didn't open the door gently when he found it unlocked but slammed it around on its hinges.

"What's wrong with you, Owen?" Regan asked. "I've already paid you! What do you want now?"

Owen reached into his breast pocket for the envelope of counterfeit money and threw it onto the coffee table in front of Regan. "How could you be so stupid as to try to give me counterfeit money?"

"I don't know what you're talking about. These look fine to me."

"Don't play me for a fool. Look at the serial numbers! Each denomination has the same serial number!"

"I don't know why these bills are counterfeit, but I'll get to the bottom of it."

"Why should I believe anything you tell me?" Owen asked.

"It's not my fault that you dropped Booth's note when you stabbed a police officer that night at Ford's Theatre."

"I make no excuses for what I did then nor for what I'm about to do now." Regan raised his right arm and flicked his wrist. A small derringer pistol slid into his hand. "I'm ready to end our relationship right now," Regan said.

Owen drew his revolver a moment too late. The bullet from Regan's derringer hit him in the chest, but he managed to fire a shot as he fell.

Regan heard Owen's bullet strike the marble fireplace behind him. He stood for a moment with both relief and satisfaction. He then stared at Owen's crumpled body as Zack and Alex rushed into the room with their revolvers drawn.

"We heard shots being fired!" Zack shouted.

"It was either him or me," Regan said. "At least this is one aggravation I won't have to deal with any longer."

"What should we do with him?" Zack asked.

"Get rid of the body and clean up the blood."

"What about the Booth note you told us about?" Alex asked.

"We'll have to look for it at Owen's house. Then I'll need to talk to Rita about the counterfeit money she gave me for the healing cup."

CHAPTER 21

RENEWAL AND REVELATION

Rita positioned her wheelchair in her bedroom so that she faced a long dresser with a large mirror above it. The mirror had been intentionally tilted downward so she could see herself in her wheelchair. She looked at her haggard and disappointed image in the mirror and wondered why the healing cup, which sat prominently on the dresser next to an empty washbasin, had not healed her.

Life seemed so incredibly unfair. The war had made her a widow, and the covert deceit of Regan and Booth had made her a coconspirator in the Lincoln assassination. She knew she couldn't change anything, but her mounting despair made her wonder if she had a life worth living.

An instant later, she turned her wheelchair toward her closed bedroom door when she heard loud voices and a commotion outside the door. The disturbance became obvious when Regan shoved the door open and pushed Eva aside. "I see you've made an early start this morning, Regan," Rita said.

"You know why I'm here."

"Whatever do you mean?"

"Don't be coy with me, Rita. You know it's about the counterfeit money you gave me."

"I was desperate, Regan. Besides, what about the healing cup you gave me that didn't work?"

"I never promised it would do anything for you."

"Nevertheless, I'd say we're just about even. I got a cup that didn't work, and you got counterfeit money."

"I don't like being deceived! You still owe me real money!"

"I don't have it, Regan!"

Before she could react, she instantly felt the pain from Regan's slap across her face. Though momentarily stunned, she instinctively touched her cheek and now felt blood oozing from the corner of her mouth.

"Then you better figure out a way to get it, or else."

"Or else what, Regan? Are you going to put an old lady in a wheelchair out of her misery?"

"You didn't need to hit her," Eva said. "Can't you take pity on a woman in wheelchair?"

"It's all right, Eva. I probably deserved it. Put some water in that fake healing cup on the dresser and get me a handkerchief. There're some old ones in the top tray of that old trunk over there that I never bothered to unpack. There's no need to bloody the good linen handkerchiefs in my dresser."

"Certainly, Mother," Eva said.

When Eva returned with water in the healing cup, Rita took a sip from the healing cup while watching Eva open the trunk. Eva hurriedly snatched one of the neatly stacked handkerchiefs next to a Bible. At first, Rita couldn't see a letter that had been underneath the Bible, but then saw Eva remove it from the trunk. She started to ask Eva about the letter but suddenly groaned and began to tremble.

"What's wrong with her?" Regan asked.

"I don't know! I've never seen her like this. It's as if she's having some kind of seizure. I don't know what to do!"

After a brief moment, the trembling stopped. Rita lost her grip on the healing cup. When it fell from her hand and hit the floor, the cup and its contents disintegrated into a pile of dust and then disappeared entirely. Then, without warning, Rita stared straight ahead and began to rise from her chair.

"Your own blood must have been the missing ingredient!" Eva said.

"You're right, child. It did work! It's an absolute miracle, but where did the cup go?"

"It disintegrated when it hit the floor. Then it disappeared. The blood on your mouth has also disappeared."

"There's obviously something truly magic here that we don't understand, but thank goodness it did work," Rita said.

"I'm so happy for you, Mother. It's truly a miracle to have you whole again."

Regan snatched the letter from Eva and started to open it, but Eva snatched it back.

"It's from Father. Here, you read it, Mother."

Before Rita opened the letter, she kicked her wheelchair against the wall.

"I guess I won't need that damn thing anymore."

"What does Father say in his letter?" Eva asked.

Rita lifted the eyeglasses chained to her neck and began reading the letter.

> *My dearest Rita,*
> *If you're reading this letter, it must be that I'm no longer able to be with you. There are no words to express how much I love you, but you need to remain strong in my absence. I can't put a price on our love for each other, but I'd like you to know that the Confederate treasury is located in the floor of the caboose connected to the train*

that I had burned in Richmond. If you're able to retrieve
the treasury, it will be yours since I'm the last of my men
surely to be killed by the Union. Take care of our child and
give it all the love that I won't be able to.

With all my love,
David

Rita had barely finished reading the letter when Regan reached over and snagged it once again.

"I don't believe it. The Confederate treasury! That's impossible!"

"Now, Regan, we've got something to talk about instead of a mere ten thousand dollars. After all this time, can you imagine that the entire wealth of the Confederate treasury was hidden under the floor of a caboose?"

"It sounds fantastic, Mother, but there must be hundreds or even thousands of trains. Where would we even start to look?"

"She's right, you know," Regan said. "It'd be like trying to find a diamond on a white sand beach."

"It may not be as difficult as you might think."

"What do you mean?" Regan asked.

"Well, just before my husband was killed, I saw the burning of the train that I was supposed to take out of Richmond. Now I know why my husband was so secretive about the large number of bags being loaded into a compartment in the floor of the caboose. Don't you see? Those bags must still contain the Confederate treasury that my husband referred to in the letter! He then burned the train to make it useless to the Union so it wouldn't be taken anywhere."

"That makes sense that they wanted to keep the train in Richmond," Regan said. "That way, they would know exactly where it was located so they could retrieve the treasury when they needed it. Besides, why would the Union have any interest in a burned-out train or even suspect that the caboose contained the Confederate treasury? That sounds pretty clever to me."

"Exactly, Regan. Think about it for a moment," Rita said. "No one else would ever want to take a burned-out train either. My hope is that it's still abandoned in Richmond."

"It certainly sounds like it might be possible."

"My thoughts exactly," Rita said. Her attention now turned to Regan's two sons, Zack and Alex, who suddenly burst into the bedroom.

"We found the note," Zack said. "Of all places, it was under his desk pad. We couldn't believe how easy it was to find. It's almost as if he wanted someone to find it."

"Really? Somehow, I smell a setup," Regan said.

"It doesn't matter," Rita said. "It's better that we found it rather than someone else. Burn it and get rid of it once and for all." After she handed Regan the note, he lit it and dropped it into the empty washbasin to burn.

CHAPTER 22

A MISSED OPPORTUNITY

Rita didn't need a ramp anymore as a means of getting a wheelchair up to the passenger platform of the Philadelphia train depot. An early morning crowd filled the platform for the next train to Richmond. Rita, Eva, Regan, and his two sons stood solemnly since they couldn't find any available seats on the wooden slatted benches. When a train finally puffed its way to a stop next to the platform, a black porter exited the depot office.

Rita immediately recognized the porter as Ezra, her former slave. She remembered their carriage ride from Richmond to Washington after she last saw her husband. She also remembered that Regan had given Ezra one of his business cards and had directed him to the railroad depot to look for work since Rita had released him from being her slave.

"Miss Rita and Mister Regan, I almost didn't recognize the two of you," Ezra said.

"It's good to see you again, Ezra," Rita said. "It's been such a long time."

Ezra flashed a broad smile, showing a mouthful of white teeth. "I'm now the chief porter of this here train, and I'll be glad to help you in any way I can."

"I want to congratulate you, Ezra," Regan said. "I'm glad to see you made the most of your efforts at the train depot."

"I owe you and Miss Rita for the chance you gave me. Let me have your tickets and I'll lead you to your seats."

"By the way, Ezra," Rita said. "I'd like you to meet my daughter, Eva."

"And I'd like you to meet my two sons, Zack and Alex," Regan said.

"My, my, you both have such fine-looking children," Ezra said. "I'll take their tickets too so I can be sure you all sit together."

With intermediate stops in Baltimore, Washington, and Fredericksburg, the train ride to Richmond took most of the day. Upon arrival, Rita now saw Richmond much differently from the city she had left near the end of the war. It had grown significantly, and it seemed to have a more vibrant atmosphere than she remembered. However, the train depot had not changed much over the years. They found the train master's office and entered it.

"May I help you folks?" Gabe Caldwell, the train master, inquired.

Rita spoke first. "I know it's been a long time ago, but do you remember a train that was burned near the end of the war?"

"You must be talking about the old five-oh-nine."

"I don't know about the number, but it could have been the five-oh-nine," Rita said.

"I've been here since the war began. It's the only train I remember being burned. Besides, who'd want to do a fool thing like that these days?"

"Where's the train now?" Regan asked. "I didn't see a train outside that might look like it."

"It's funny that you should ask. Some yahoos in fancy duds up and bought the old train a few months ago."

"What did they do with it?" Regan asked.

"Well, they hired some locals to rebuild the superstructures on each car and then hired an old German engineer, Helmut Gerhard, to get the locomotive running again."

"Do you know where they might have taken it?" Regan asked.

"Not really, but they had Canterbury Circus painted on the sides of some of the cars."

"That circus was just in Philadelphia several weeks ago," Zack said.

"And I saw a circus poster at the Philadelphia train depot," Alex said. "It said it would be back in Philadelphia the day after tomorrow."

"I'd like to see more of Richmond," Eva said. "Can we stay a little longer?"

"No, dear," Rita said. "We need to take the next train back to Philadelphia as soon as possible."

CHAPTER 23

THE TREASURE

Adam sat next to Edward and Merlin in the Canterbury Circus grandstands at one of the evening performances. He noticed that Edward reserved most of his enthusiastic applause for the conclusion of Ivy's acrobatic performance but that Merlin seemed to enjoy everything he saw, especially the elephants and lions. He also noticed that Merlin seemed equally awed by the breathtaking and death-defying performances of the tightrope walkers and the trapeze artists. He had to smile at Merlin's almost childlike excitement and wondered if he'd ever seen a circus before.

The performances went on flawlessly for nearly an hour, until Adam heard the distant crack of three gunshots somewhere outside the tent. He looked in Uncle George's direction near the tent entrance and saw him wave his hand. He sensed that Uncle George wanted to talk to him. He stood up and moved toward Uncle George, with Edward and Merlin behind him.

The people in the audience became uneasy and began chatting

with each other even though the performances continued without pause. It appeared that the performers had trained themselves to ignore distractions since it could affect their concentration.

"It sounded as if it came from the direction of the train," Uncle George said. "I think the three of you better check it out while I have Grant try to calm the crowd. I'll have him say that the clowns were just practicing their act."

Adam led the charge to exit the circus tent and ran toward a lantern held by Helmut, the locomotive engineer, who stood near the caboose. Adam and Edward both drew revolvers when Helmut waved his arm to bring them closer. When Adam reached Helmut, he grabbed Helmut's arm. "Have you been hurt, Helmut?"

"No, I'm all right, but I think I scared them off."

"What happened?" Edward asked.

"I saw a light in the caboose when I was making my rounds. When I looked in the window of the caboose's front door, I saw three men and two women. That's when I sounded the alarm with the three shots."

Adam took Helmut's lantern and entered the caboose ahead of Edward and Merlin. "It doesn't look like anything has been disturbed," Edward said.

"All except for one thing," Merlin said. "That corner of the carpet is curled up like someone was trying to pull it back."

"You're right, Merlin," Adam said. "Help me with the carpet, Edward."

"They're just iron plates," Helmut said. "There shouldn't be anything of interest under them."

"What I do find interesting is that they don't seem to be welded to anything," Adam said. "I want to see for myself what's under them. Do we have any pry bars on the train?"

"I have some in the engine compartment," Helmut said. "I'll go get them."

It took several minutes to retrieve the pry bars from the locomotive. Adam helped Edward pry one of the plates up just enough so the edge of the plate could be lifted and flipped against the side of the caboose.

In the new opening, Adam saw rows of bags. He reached down to untie one of the bags and brought up a handful of Confederate coins.

"I don't bloody believe it!" Edward said. "There must be millions of dollars in gold and silver coins in these bags!"

"I would speculate that this represents the entire Confederate treasury," Adam said.

"And I can't believe we've been carrying around this hoard of money all these months without ever knowing it," Helmut said.

"We need to put everything back in place for now so the police and the Treasury Department can be notified," Adam said and then shook his head. "It's too bad it has to go to a bunch of Washington bureaucrats who will probably squander it on some worthless government programs."

"All may not be lost," Edward said. "Since it was found on circus property, the circus may realize a significant finder's fee."

"Wouldn't Uncle George be thrilled to hear about that?" Adam said.

A moment later, a wagon and a carriage pulled up outside the caboose. A police wagon held several policemen, and the carriage held Inspector Fagan.

"I heard shots and came to investigate," Fagan said. "I wanted to see if anyone had been hurt."

"We found a large sum of money in the caboose," Adam said.

"How much money?"

"Enough for your entire police force to consider retirement. Your men need to guard it until the Treasury Department is contacted and can send agents to pick it up."

"I agree," Fagan said. "I'll personally get someone from the Treasury Department out of bed to handle the situation while my men are deployed around it."

"Thank you, Inspector," Adam said. "You're a good man."

"I'm just doing my job."

CHAPTER 24

A MOMENT OF
DISTRESS AND
THEN HOPE

Regan stood in front of his marble fireplace while staring up at a portrait of his late wife above the fireplace. He then gazed at his two sons sitting in padded chairs on either side of a coffee table. He repeatedly recounted the vision of the train and the treasure of a lifetime in the train's caboose. The thought of almost holding even a piece of the treasure in his hands and then losing it swirled in his mind with an endless procession of images that faded then reappeared.

"The newspaper says that the Confederate treasury was accidently discovered by a Pinkerton detective and a Lloyd's detective," Alex said. "The treasury is believed to be valued at several million dollars and is to be turned over to the United States Treasury Department."

"They must be the ones that've been watching our every move," Zack said.

"That means that we've got to be extra careful now," Regan said.

"For sure. We've lost Laura Morgan, our contact at the museum," Zack said. "There's no way I could convince her to help us again."

"She'd be useless to us now anyway since they've somehow figured out our scheme to steal artifacts from the museum using shipping documents."

"I've seen something at the museum that may help us branch out from stealing only artifacts," Alex said.

"What's that, Alex?" Regan asked.

"There are two Egyptian necklaces, the Eye of Horus necklace and the Isis magical necklace."

"I've seen those necklaces," Zack said. "I saw nothing special about them."

"Egyptian legend has it that whenever the magical necklace is placed around the neck of Osiris in the presence of someone wearing the Eye of Horus, an impenetrable aura appears around the wearer of the Eye of Horus."

"That's absurd," Zack said. "Your fantasies are getting the best of you. Besides, Osiris doesn't exist."

"But his statue does!"

"Let's stop our quibbling," Regan said. "After how I saw the healing cup totally heal Rita, I'm willing to consider anything that doesn't seem possible. Let's get to the bottom of this argument to see if it's really possible."

"I think both of you are crazy," Zack said.

"Nonetheless, I'd like you and Alex to put this impossibility to the test."

That evening, Zack managed to pick the lock on the side door of the museum, and he eased inside, Alex close behind him. A display alcove near the door allowed them to hide their presence. Zack pulled out a coin and flipped it into the adjacent hallway to attract the night watchman. The light of a full moon streaming into the museum through a skylight allowed the guard to see the coin clearly. The skylights allowed lighting that was more natural during the daylight hours for better viewing of the exhibits. When the guard bent over to pick up the coin, Zack sneaked up behind him and knocked him out with his revolver.

"He'll be out for hours. It'll now be safe for us to do whatever we want to do," Alex said.

Zack led them into the Egyptian exhibit with no hesitation. He lifted the glass case, removed the Eye of Horus necklace, and placed it around his neck. At the same time, he saw Alex open another glass case and remove Isis's magical necklace. Zack then positioned himself in front of the Osiris statue. He stood like a man in front of a firing squad, with his feet together and his arms at his sides. He then gave a nod to Alex to place Isis's magical necklace around Osiris's stone neck. Instantly, two beams of white light streamed from Osiris's eyes and struck the Eye of Horus amulet.

"Are you all right?" Alex asked.

Zack looked down and touched the necklace's amulet. "I'm fine. I just felt a little pressure against my chest."

Alex tried to touch him but jumped back and violently shook his hand. "Wow, it really worked!"

Zack spread his arms in jubilation. "I have great expectations with this new power! We should leave this place so I can try it out."

"Perhaps you should take the necklace off for a moment to see if the aura temporarily goes away."

"Why would I want to leave myself unprotected?"

"Because there may be situations where you may not want to give away your identity as an invincible criminal," Alex said.

"I see your point." Zack removed the necklace and saw that Alex didn't have the same reaction as he did before.

"You shouldn't need to wear the necklace until you're ready to actually use it," Alex said.

CHAPTER 25
A TRIAL RUN

The next day, few customers milled about the Hargrove Bank when it became midday. On this day, nothing seemed particularly unusual. One customer stood at the stand-up table, and one customer stood at the teller window next to Eva's window. The bank manager reclined in his chair while he read the newspaper and munched on an apple.

Dan Covington entered the bank and immediately walked to Eva's window. He usually had lunch with Eva when he had a break during an investigation. Ever since he had saved her from a speeding carriage, they had developed a close relationship.

Just as Dan started to leave with Eva, Zack and Alex O'Brien rushed into the bank with their masks up and their revolvers drawn. All the people in the bank raised their hands. Dan and Eva backed up against the front of Eva's teller window when Zack pointed his revolver at them. Zack tossed a bag to Eva. "Start collecting money from the teller drawers!"

Alex opened the gate in front of the bank supervisor's desk and moved in front of the bank supervisor while pointing a revolver at him. "Start opening the vault!"

Dan took advantage of Alex's distraction with the bank manager. In an instant, he reached to his shoulder holster and drew the revolver his father had finally entrusted to him. He fired a shot at Zack, but the bullet only created a spark in front of Zack and then fell unblemished to the floor and rolled to a stop.

"You've made a very foolish mistake, my friend."

When Zack fired a shot at Dan, Dan dropped his revolver, grabbed his shoulder, and leaned against the teller window. He managed to hold himself up while blood oozed between his fingers. He took a handkerchief Eva retrieved from her purse and pressed it against the wound. When the bank manager finally opened the vault, he saw Alex throw a bag to the bank manager.

"Fill it up with as much as it'll hold!"

Zack snatched Eva's bag with the money from the teller drawers. "Hurry up! We need to get out of here!" Zack said.

After Alex grabbed the bank manager's bag, Dan saw the two robbers rush to the front door and leave with their pistols still drawn. As Dan's eyes began to close, he slumped to the floor.

"I need help!" Eva exclaimed. "Dan needs a doctor before he loses any more blood!"

CHAPTER 26
A TIME TO REGROUP

Charles Covington's mood changed dramatically when he heard that his son, Dan, had been wounded during a bank robbery. When he became convinced of Dan's safe recovery, he angrily returned to his office from the hospital. He then paid a young boy, who often helped him with relaying messages, to summon everyone to his office, including Fagan.

"We're going to make every effort to get to the bottom of this situation and find out who shot Dan," Fagan said.

"I'm sure you will, Inspector, because I've got a great deal of confidence in the police." Charles looked at Merlin and smiled. "I'm glad Merlin was able to attend. We'll need his help with this unusual situation."

"I certainly hope I can help. I've done some reading about Egyptian mythology, but it's unbelievable that some of it has actually come true."

"I don't know anything about Egyptian myths, but something strange is definitely going on," Fagan said.

"I agree. Something beyond our understanding definitely deflected Dan's bullet," Charles said.

"How in the world is such a thing possible?" Fagan asked. "An invisible wall that stops bullets? There must be some logical explanation!"

"The Egyptians were incredibly intelligent," Merlin said. "Their understanding of things unknown to us should not be underestimated."

"But how can we possibly oppose something that we know absolutely nothing about?" Charles asked.

"First of all, I suspect that the thieves are career criminals, not Egyptian enthusiasts gone mad with a desire for power," Merlin said.

"If that's true, then how did the thieves learn about the Egyptian myths?" Charles asked.

"They must have learned about its supposed mythical powers at the Museum of Archaeology and Anthropology," Edward said.

"I think most Egyptians know the stories about Osiris, Isis, and Seth, but I don't think they take the stories seriously," Merlin said. "They're just ancient tales that have existed over the centuries. Unfortunately, they've become so intertwined with Egypt's true history that some individuals actually have a misguided belief in the gods and thrive on the mystery and intrigue that the stories create."

"I'm sorry, but I just don't believe in magic," Charles said. "This thing has to be stopped before anyone else is hurt or even killed!"

"I have a suggestion," Merlin said.

"Please go on, Merlin," Charles said.

"Since we know bullets won't stop them, we need some way to temporarily restrain them until they can be put behind bars. Maybe a net could be rigged above them, but there'd have to be something extremely irresistible to entice them under the net."

"I don't know of anything that might work," Adam said. "What could we possibly use?"

"The daughter of Khedive Nuru, the current ruler of Egypt, is visiting Philadelphia while her father meets with the president in Washington," Charles said. "I've been told that she wears a necklace that was supposedly worn by Cleopatra."

"That would certainly be enticing enough," Merlin said.

"Is there anything I can do, Father?" Dan asked.

"Yes. You can go talk to the curator at the Museum of Archaeology and Anthropology about setting up a net. To me, that sounds like the logical place to make the capture."

"We still need some way to notify the thieves," Charles said. "I'll talk to Catherine about creating a newspaper article concerning the display of the Cleopatra necklace at the museum."

CHAPTER 27

THE CONFRONTATION

Obviously, the museum had to close before the net could be installed. Its lightness allowed it to be hung by small hooks, but it retained enough strength to entrap the thieves. A single small rope attached to each corner of the net and threaded through the hooks held the corners at their highest points. A single center hook in the center of the room held up the center of the net to prevent it from drooping. Bricks placed over the free ends of the corner ropes temporarily held the corners of the net in place.

After they'd finished this, Charles watched Felix Franklin, the museum curator, move a glass-covered display case containing the Cleopatra necklace beneath the center of the net. He, along with Adam and Edward, then positioned themselves behind empty display cases in each corner of the room next to their ropes. Merlin positioned himself with the fourth rope in a nearby display alcove containing a bust of Anubis, the god of the underworld. Charles hadn't said anything earlier when he saw Merlin remove Isis's magical necklace from the Osiris statue because he didn't see why it had anything to do with what would soon be happening. He could only speculate that Merlin had his reasons. With everything and everyone in place, he signaled Felix to turn off all the lamps. Total darkness now enveloped the room and effectively hid the net and all that held it in place.

Charles knew the thieves had to come that evening because the newspaper article stated that the Cleopatra necklace would only be on display the next day. Everything seemed to be ready, but how could he be sure it would actually work? With no way to defeat the aura, he had no choice but to have some method to snag the thieves before they could effectively retaliate.

Silence permeated the room, with only occasional small talk to pass the time. A clock ticked away the boredom. Only the anticipation of the coming actions seemed to offset it. At the moment, nothing seemed as important to Charles as stopping the thieves in their tracks and putting them behind bars.

The creak of a side entrance door shattered the intense boredom each of them had endured. Charles, Adam, Edward, and Merlin each grabbed their corner ropes and as silently as possible lifted and removed the retaining bricks from their ropes. The light shuffling of multiple footsteps preceded the intruders into a darkened room where their captors waited. A lantern lit by one of the intruders and placed on the display case revealed two men standing in front of the display case.

Charles shouted a command. "Release the ropes!"

The corners of the net dropped down and draped over the two men. A shower of sparks further illuminated the room as the net made contact with the aura. Suddenly, a stream of pure white light crossed the room and contacted the Eye of Horus amulet. The sparks instantly stopped, and Charles saw both men struggling against the net to raise their revolvers. Charles shouted another command. "Drop your weapons or I'll shoot!" When the men ignored his command, Charles wounded one of the men while Adam fired a shot and hit the other man in the shoulder.

"We did it!" Edward said.

"Yes, we did, but where'd that beam of light come from?" Charles asked.

They all searched around the room until Charles saw Merlin grinning broadly and patting the bust of Anubis on top of the head, with the Isis magical necklace around Anubis's neck.

"It never hurts to have a little backup, don't you think?"

"Is this part of your supposed wizardry, Merlin?" Charles asked.

"Not at all. I merely assumed that Anubis, the god of the underworld, might have something to say about this magical aura. You have to give me credit for something since the rest of you did all the hard work."

"You're absolutely amazing, Merlin," Adam said.

"And you seem to have the magic of a wizard," Edward said.

A few days later, Charles met with Adam in John and Ann's kitchen after the police had completed a thorough and intense interrogation of the O'Brien brothers.

"Zack O'Brien wouldn't talk, but Alex O'Brien finally broke down and told everything. I suppose he had a guilty conscience," Charles said.

"Well, what'd he say?" Adam asked.

"He told them that during their first attempt at robbing the Hargrove Bank, he shot your father when your father shot Zack in the right leg. He further said that he hadn't intended to shoot anyone except it was a reflex action to further protect Zack."

"Finally, I now know what really happened to my father. That only leaves the clearing of my father's name."

"There's been some progress there too."

"What do you mean?"

"A note from John Wilkes Booth to Regan O'Brien that implicates both Regan and Rita Sims in the Lincoln assassination was found under the desk pad in Owen Park's office at the *Philadelphia Inquirer.*"

"Then Regan and Rita were the two people that drew my father away from the stairs to the Lincoln box at Ford's Theatre with a fake fainting spell!"

"That corroborates your father's story. I'm sure William Pinkerton will now plan on giving you an apology for your father's firing."

"It will be an apology well received by me, but when will Regan and Rita be arrested?"

"That's already being worked on by Inspector Fagan."

"I can hardly wait."

"While we're here, I want to talk to you about something else."

"What do you mean, Charles?"

"It's about Catherine. She needs you as much as you need her."

"I know, and I think I've finally come to terms with Tim's death and her rejection of me for allowing her twin brother to be killed."

"You need to talk to her. It's the only thing that will make both of you whole again."

"I agree. It's long overdue. You know, I haven't been able to stop thinking about her since we separated. For once, time seems to be on our side to heal our wounds."

Charles grabbed Adam's shoulder. "It's never easy to forgive, but you have to let her try."

CHAPTER 28

REGAN'S ARREST AND THEN A SURPRISE

Regan O'Brien sat in one of the padded chairs in front of his marble fireplace. He stared unblinkingly at the flames that repeatedly licked the air. He couldn't believe his two sons had been arrested, but he also couldn't think of any way to help them. With despair, he grabbed a bottle of laudanum he had placed on the coffee table next to his chair and took a healthy swig before sitting back with his eyes closed.

Except for the crackling of the fire, silence filled every corner of the room. He wished he could be somewhere else, but he felt trapped in a life with no future and no place to go. A life of dishonesty hadn't really gotten him very far, but he couldn't change anything now. What did he have to look forward to? The world seemed to be closing in on him without mercy. He knew the laudanum might temporarily change his viewpoint of life, but he also knew that he'd have to return to reality.

Inspector Fagan loudly rapped his knuckles on the front door of Regan's house and spoke with a gruff voice of urgency. "Open up, O'Brien! This is the Metropolitan Police!"

"Come on in, Inspector," Regan said. "The door's unlocked. I recognize your voice from our last meeting. What do you want? What reason do you have for being here?"

Fagan entered the house followed by two police officers, Charles, Adam, Edward, and Merlin. He could see that Regan didn't intend to get up since he could still see the top of Regan's head above the back of a padded chair. As such, he decided to walk around the chair and face Regan. "You're under arrest, Regan O'Brien, for conspiracy to assassinate the president of the United States."

"You have no proof!"

"On the contrary, we have a handwritten and signed note from John Wilkes Booth to you that implicates both you and Rita Sims."

"That's impossible!"

"I think not. It was found under the desk pad on Owen Park's desk at the *Philadelphia Inquirer*. You need to stand up and come with us."

"You have no proof that I was even there!"

"As a matter of fact, there's a policeman that's recovered from being stabbed by you that night. He's ready to identify you."

"Do you think I'm going to let you make me into a spectacle at a public hanging?"

Before the two officers could get close enough to grab Regan's arms and before Fagan could react, Fagan saw a small derringer appear in Regan's right hand. He then watched in horror as Regan raised the derringer and fired it into the side of his head. "He's done for. You two need to go get an ambulance."

As all this went on, no one noticed that Merlin had stepped outside the house. He carefully made mental notes of the position and characteristics of each exterior wall. He then came inside and did the same careful examination. "Something doesn't add up."

"What do you mean, Merlin?" Charles asked.

"The back side of the fireplace isn't visible from the outside."

"Are you suspecting a hidden room?"

"Quite possibly." He removed a lamp from the fireplace mantel and lit it but left the lamp's glass chimney off. He slowly moved the flame across the front of the fireplace until he saw it flicker at the junction of the fireplace and a bookshelf. "Here. It's here. We need to push against the side of the bookcase."

Charles, with the help of Adam and Edward, easily slid the bookcase away from the fireplace. Even with poor lighting, he could see the golden glow of the seven-inch solid gold figurine of the Egyptian deity Amun-Re on a pedestal.

"You've done it again, Merlin," Charles said. "Is there any limit to your abilities?"

"It's merely deductive logic, nothing more."

"You'd make a fine detective if you ever decided to be one."

"I'm afraid that I'm a bit too old to pursue that profession, but I've enjoyed watching you fine gentlemen at work. You must find it very satisfying to unravel the clues and find the truth."

Meanwhile, Adam turned his attention to a well-worn book beneath the coffee table and picked it up. He opened it and began flipping through the yellowed pages.

"What do you have there, Adam?" Edward asked.

"It appears to be a ship's logbook. I think it may have belonged to Captain Kidd."

"You can't be serious! Captain Kidd? Really?"

"Captain Kidd was a rogue privateer whom the British Royal Navy hated," Merlin said. "When he learned that he was going to be considered a pirate, he started hiding his treasures to use as leverage during his trial."

"What eventually happened to him?" Edward asked.

"To my recollection of what I've read about him, he was tried and convicted in England of five counts of piracy and the murder of a crewman. They then hanged him twice since the hangman's rope broke during the first attempt."

"I noticed that several pages have been torn out of the logbook, Merlin. What do you make of that?"

"I speculate that Captain Kidd did that himself to hide the location of his final treasure."

"It appears that the O'Briens had some unfinished business," Charles said. "Are the three of you thinking about treasure hunting?"

"The thought did cross my mind," Adam said. "Besides, I remember the night when Helmut scared someone off with his warning shots. I suspect that it was the O'Briens who tried to get their hands on the Confederate treasury. What would be more satisfying than to find something else they couldn't get their hands on?"

"I agree," Edward said. "We need to do this."

"I think it's a jolly good idea," Merlin said. "I wouldn't miss it for the world."

"If we could somehow find the missing pages, we might find the treasure," Adam said. "We just don't have any clue as to where to look."

"There's an old seaman who takes care of the Turtle Rock Lighthouse, which is just north of the city," Fagan said. "I've heard from others that he claims that his great-grandfather was Captain Kidd's second-in-command."

"How about you, Edward?" Adam asked. "Do you think you could convince your supervisor to let you leave the drudgery of crime fighting for a while? I'm sure Charles wouldn't mind if I did, would you, Charles?"

"I can't speak for Edward's supervisor, but I think the two of you have earned some time off."

"And how about you, Merlin?" Adam asked. "What're your plans? You know, we might need your assistance along the way."

"I'm thoroughly fascinated with the idea. You certainly can count on my being available."

CHAPTER 29

THE LIGHTHOUSE

Due to the slight remoteness of the lighthouse, Adam hired a special carriage to take them there and promised an even larger tip to the driver if he picked them up later in the day for their return trip. Adam suspected that the trip might take slightly longer since they would be traveling through the heart of the city in the late morning.

The carriage driver headed northward with neither hesitation nor reservation. He soon confronted a maze of streets and intersections. With no rules for traffic flow, he constantly weaved around merchants with their carts filled with a wide assortment of produce, fresh fish, flowers, and merchandise of all types. He even came upon a horse-drawn trolley but passed it with ease. Along with this seemingly normal activity of the streets, the aroma of freshly baked bread mixed with the odors of leather harnesses, horses, and dust-laden brick and wooden structures filled the air.

At the next intersection, the driver turned westward toward the eastern bank of the Schuylkill River. He continued in that direction until he reached a road paralleling the riverbank and then turned north again. Farther north, he encountered the Market Street Bridge but passed it by and continued even farther north until he reached Boathouse Row. Looking to his right, Adam saw elegant mansions with column-supported porticos and expansive tree-covered lawns. To his left, he saw numerous boathouses that contained racing sculls and yachts to satisfy the recreational appetites of the wealthy. Once past the mansions and boathouses, he saw the Turtle Rock Lighthouse perched at the end of Kelly Drive.

As the carriage came closer, Adam could clearly see the hexagonal-shaped lantern room at the top of the lighthouse. It had an octagonal-shaped walkway around it. Obviously, the lighthouse overlooked the river with the purpose of aiding river traffic around a bend in the river.

Upon reaching the lighthouse, he saw the lighthouse keeper calmly sitting in a rocking chair on a small porch while puffing on his pipe.

"I'm Adam Blake, and these are my friends, Edward Frost and Merlin Pendragon. We'd like to talk with you for a few minutes if you wouldn't mind."

"By all means. I'm Roman Atherton. You're the first guests I've had in some time."

"You must get kind of lonely up here," Adam said. "You don't seem to have many close neighbors."

"Sometimes I see them, but I'm used to being alone. At sea, you don't have any neighbors either, except for your mates."

"We won't take much of you time," Adam said. "May we come in?"

"I don't see why not. I don't have much in the way of comforts, but as I'm kind of a hermit, I don't need much."

As they entered the house, Adam heard the wooden floor creak slightly until he reached a circular woven carpet that covered nearly the entire room. To the right, he saw a couch covered in a green fabric, and just above the couch, he saw a pistol mounted in a glass-covered case. To the left of the couch, he saw an open doorway that seemed to lead into a dining area and kitchen. To the left side of the doorway, he saw a soot-smudged fireplace. A large painting of a ship hung above the fireplace, and candles in brass candleholders sat on the mantel on either side of the painting. Just to the left of the fireplace, he saw a small wooden replica of the ship in the painting. Finally, to the left of the model, he saw two padded chairs with a small table between them and a small jewelry box on the table.

After everyone entered the room, Adam gave Roman the logbook. "We didn't know if this belonged to you, but we wanted you to have it."

"I thought it was lost forever! Where did you find it? There was a break-in at the lighthouse a few months ago! This was the only thing that was missing. They must have wanted it to find Captain Kidd's missing treasure!"

"We didn't know about the break-in, but we did see that some pages had been torn out."

"The missing pages! They're the key to finding the treasure!"

Edward reached over the couch and took the pistol from the glass-covered case. "I've never actually seen one of these," he said.

"Captain Kidd gave it to my great-grandfather when Kidd was arrested. Obviously, it hasn't been fired in nearly two hundred years."

"Here, Adam," Edward said. "You may want to see this."

While distracted by the details of the ship model, Adam didn't readily notice Edward trying to toss him the pistol, which he then missed catching. He thought Edward must have misjudged the lightness of the pistol, which fell to the floor with an obvious thump against the woven carpet.

"Oh God, I must be bloody daft, Roman," Edward said. "I thought Adam might have wanted to see it for himself, so I tried to toss it to him. Unfortunately, it looks like part of the pistol's grip came loose."

Roman carefully picked up the pistol and removed a small cloth-wrapped object from the handle. He then gave the pistol back to Edward. With a mixture of curiosity and anticipation, he removed the cloth. Nothing could describe his excitement. "It's the key! It's the key!"

No one seemed to know anything about the key, but they stood ready to back away from Roman if he came toward them. He soon showed his intentions when he turned around and stepped toward the small table with the small jewelry box on it.

Roman nervously inserted the key into the jewelry box's small keyhole and slowly turned the key until he heard a discernable click. The rusted hinges on the jewelry box resisted as he slowly opened the lid. Disappointment and frustration replaced jubilation when he stared into the box's stark emptiness. "I really thought the missing pages would be inside. Now I think they'll never be found."

"Let's not panic," Merlin said. "I've seen these puzzle boxes before. I suspect the box's true mystery is yet to be solved."

Merlin picked up the box and examined every aspect of it. The box's sides seemed unusually thick for a box this size. He closed the lid and turned the box upside down. "The key also may have unlocked a mechanism that controls the positions of the box's feet."

He pushed on each of the feet with moderate force until one of the feet moved to the side. The other three feet instantly moved to another position. He grabbed the sides of the box and carefully lifted an outer shell from the rest of the box. He couldn't help celebrating his success and raised his hands with great fanfare. "Mystery solved!"

"Once again, Merlin, you never cease to amaze us," Adam said.

Merlin looked away and wiggled his fingers as if playing an imaginary piano. "It must be the magic in my fingers."

With haste, Roman gingerly lifted a square object wrapped in waxed paper from the dismantled jewelry box. He began peeling off the waxed paper.

"The waxed paper keeps air and moisture out to reduce the amount of deterioration," Merlin said.

After Roman finished removing the waxed paper and unfolded the now-exposed yellowed pages, his exuberance returned. "It's the missing pages!" His eyes continued to dart from side to side in an effort to absorb the meaning of each word. "It says Captain Kidd's ship was anchored just off of Plum Island!"

"There're actually several Plum Islands," Merlin said. "The one near Gardiners Island is the most likely one because one of Captain Kidd's treasures was buried and later removed from there."

"The missing pages do give directions on how to find the treasure, but we may need Merlin's help to understand them," Roman said.

"Roman, is there someone who can take care of the light while we travel for a few days to Plum Island?" Adam asked.

Roman touched his chin in thought. "There's one person who lives nearby and sometimes comes by to look at the light. I'm sure he'd be thrilled to help out."

"Good. Then we'll leave as soon as possible."

CHAPTER 30

TREASURE HUNTING

They began the longest part of their journey by boarding a train from Philadelphia to Staten Island, New York. From Staten Island, they took the Staten Island Ferry into Manhattan and then crossed the Brooklyn Bridge by carriage into Brooklyn. From Brooklyn, they boarded a train that eventually connected with the Long Island Rail Road. This train took them the full length of Long Island until they reached Greenport, New York, on the north fork of Long Island. Since rail service ended at this point, they took a carriage to the Orient Point Ferry, which took them to Plum Island. After leaving the ferry landing on Plum Island, they made their way to the Plum Island Light on the western end of Plum Island.

Adam rapped on the door of the lighthouse keeper's house and waited for several minutes. When the door finally opened with a loud creaking sound, he saw a short elderly man with a thick gray beard. Adam introduced himself and the others to Jeremiah Benoit, the lighthouse keeper. "May we come in?"

"Why, certainly," Jeremiah said. "I don't get many visitors these days, you see, but it's kind of nice to have someone to talk to once in a while."

Inside, Adam saw a rather depressing and poorly kept up room with peeling plaster on the walls and several pieces of decrepit padded furniture. He thought the main room in Roman's house looked like a palace compared to this one.

"I don't spend much time worrying about the niceties of life, but I've got enough since it's just me."

"We don't plan to stay very long, but we do need to borrow some things for a short while," Adam said.

"You must be a bunch of those treasure hunters who've come to find Captain Kidd's treasure, aren't you?"

"We hope it'll be different this time," Roman said. "My great-grandfather was Captain Kidd's second-in-command, and we've found some information about the treasure's location."

"Huh, maybe you're on to something. What do you need?"

"We need two shovels and two ropes that are about two hundred feet long," Merlin said.

"I have lots of shovels left by disgruntled treasure hunters. As for the rope, I have the lengths that you need, but they're only the small-diameter hemp type that I use for maintenance of this old lighthouse. I only ask that you don't cut either of them."

"That's sounds perfect, Jeremiah," Adam said. "Would you like to come with us?"

"No, not really. I've seen too many shattered dreams already."

"Can you tell us any myths about Captain Kidd?" Merlin asked. "I'm always interested in such things."

"I'd like to hear them too," Edward said. "I love to hear pirate stories!"

"Well, there's one story that seems to persist. It's said that Captain Kidd once anchored his ship off of Plum Island and had his men carry a heavy chest ashore."

"His men must not have cared much for carrying it any great distance," Edward said.

"Actually, they didn't have to. They captured two black slaves on the island and blindfolded them. It was their task to carry the chest to its final location and dig the hole."

"What happened to the slaves?" Edward asked. "Did either of them escape the pirates?"

"One of them escaped when they were both being brought to the ship, but the other one later washed ashore with a cannonball tied to his feet."

"I guess they didn't think they'd get much for the one slave they later killed and didn't want to search for the other one," Edward said.

"Just remember that it's only a myth and that there's probably not much truth to it."

After collecting the shovels and ropes, Merlin led them to the base of a line of boulders on the north shore. Nothing made the location unique. They just stood on a lot of sand covered with sparse, scruffy vegetation.

"Why are there boulders on the island, Merlin?" Edward asked. "There aren't any mountains nearby."

"I've read a little bit about this area," Merlin said. "The boulders are part of what's called a terminal moraine. Believe it or not, an ice sheet covered this area many thousands of years ago. When the climate became warmer, the ice sheet began to melt. Since the ice could no longer hold the boulders, they were left here on the island."

"How'd you get so smart, Merlin?" Edward said. "Most people don't read much after leaving school, except when they have to."

"I've always thought reading was one of the best ways to gain a broad knowledge of things because without knowledge, nothing meaningful can be achieved."

"Why'd you pick this location, Merlin? Is there something we're supposed to do here?" Adam asked.

"The first thing you and Edward need to do is find two iron spikes wedged in the boulders. They're going to be some distance apart. When you and Edward find them, raise your arms."

After searching for a short while, Merlin saw Adam and Edward find their rusted iron spikes among some of the smaller boulders that lay closer to where he stood than the shoreline.

When Merlin saw them raise their arms, he waved them back toward him. "You now need to tie one end of each rope to an iron spike. I'll hold both of the free ends here."

While Adam and Edward started pulling their ropes toward their iron spikes, Merlin kept the ropes from getting tangled. The lightweight ropes pulled easily but sometimes caught between the boulders.

After they had tied the ropes to the iron spikes and raised their arms, Merlin waved them back again. "The next thing you need to do is to take these free ends to the opposing iron spikes, pull the ropes taut, and tie a knot in the ropes at the locations of the opposing spikes. After you've finished this task, you'll need to bring the free knotted ends toward me and toward each of you until they meet."

"I now understand!" Roman said. "Where the knots meet is where the treasure's buried!"

"It's a rather clever and reasonably accurate way to locate the treasure without leaving any evidence of its location," Merlin said. "The ropes and the iron spikes form what's called an equilateral triangle."

Merlin saw that Adam and Edward had found a common point for the knots only a short distance behind him and Roman. The sandy spot, which had virtually no vegetation or small boulders nearby, would provide easy digging. He watched Roman rush to the spot without any prompting and repeatedly jam the heel of his boot into the soft sand to form a slight depression.

"This is it! This is where we dig!"

"Roman and I will start digging first while you and Edward take a short rest," Merlin said. "We'll then let the two of you take over. There's no way of telling how deep we'll have to go."

Even with adrenaline rushing through their veins, Merlin and Roman clearly found the digging exhausting. Only after a short time did they gratefully relinquish their shovels to the younger Adam and Edward.

After another two feet or so, they all heard Edward's shovel hit something solid. They immediately stopped digging and started brushing the sand away to determine the outline of the object. Merlin saw that Roman couldn't contain himself.

"It's a chest!"

Merlin watched Adam and Edward continue to dig around the chest until they exposed the rest of the lid and a padlock. He then watched Adam take several whacks at the rusted hasp with the end of his shovel until the hasp broke. Everyone held their breath while Adam and Edward raised the lid. The sun poured into the chest and brilliantly reflected off some of the metal surfaces. Inside the chest, they found bags of gold dust, bars of silver, Spanish dollars, rubies, diamonds, candlesticks, and low one-handled bowls or cups known as porringers.

While Roman stood stunned and speechless with a blank stare on his face, Merlin's eyes sparkled with excitement. "By Jove, it's a bloody king's ransom!"

REFLECTIONS

Adam and Merlin sat quietly next to each other on the last leg of their train trip back to Philadelphia. Adam sat next to the window and stared at the passing scenery. "Time seems to pass quickly when you don't think about it too much, Merlin. We've seen the O'Briens each meet their individual fates, we've discovered the location of the Confederate treasury, and we've even found one of Captain Kidd's buried treasures. Everything seems like a blur, like the scenery I'm watching out the window."

"If you did think about time too much, Adam, you'd worry yourself to death about what was going to happen next," Merlin said. "Time is constantly changing, and we just have to accept it. It's just like our regrets and our mistakes. You have to accept and live with those too. What you have to do is find comfort and satisfaction in the things that you've accomplished. As you know, no one's perfect, and we shouldn't try to be. We just have to live our lives as best as we can."

"Just finding a treasure would mean a life of leisure and luxury to anyone," Adam said. "It's not that I wouldn't welcome that kind of wealth, but there has to be more to life than what wealth can buy." Adam turned away from the window and looked at Merlin. "What do you value more than anything else in this world, Merlin?"

Merlin knew that he had cheated time by time traveling from the twelfth century, but he had to save himself and Gwen from the grotto prison Morgana had created. He also knew that his departure had created a void in the balance of good and evil he had shared with Morgana. He wondered if Morgana's wickedness had consumed the world he once knew. Then he wondered if Dagda, the great Celtic god, had apprenticed a new wizard to take his place.

Yet the world he now saw in the future had survived without his presence in the past. It seemed that humankind had become more learned about the world and had discarded the ancient beliefs in myths, magic, and multiple gods. Essentially, he thought, he had become obsolete, with no need to use his magic anymore. However, he had no regrets about leaving the twelfth century, except for deceiving Adam and the others about his identity. Telling them served no purpose. He just wanted to be the person they had come to accept, not some mythical intruder from the past. He smiled at Adam with a look of satisfaction. "That's the easiest question anyone has ever asked me, Adam. Without a doubt, it has to be family and friends like you, Edward, and everyone else with whom I've formed a lasting friendship. What more could anyone ask for?"

ABOUT THE AUTHOR

Harvey Hetrick, a retired engineer, uses aspects of his creativity and imagination to create a story with a unique blend of medieval intrigue, mystery, myth, magic, and buried treasure. After having earned bachelor degrees from Mississippi State University and the University of Utah, he now resides in Texas and has three daughters.

Printed in the USA
CPSIA information can be obtained
at www.ICGtesting.com
LVHW011028110823
754679LV00028B/143